GOLDEN CITY

BOOK THREE OF THE REALM TRILOGY

S R MANSSEN

First published in New Zealand in 2020 by Manssen Publishing House

ISBN   978-0-473-54400-3 (p/back)
ISBN   978-0-473-54401-0 (Epub)
ISBN   978-0-473-54402-7 (Kindle)

Orders: www.srmanssen.com

For everyone trapped in Medar

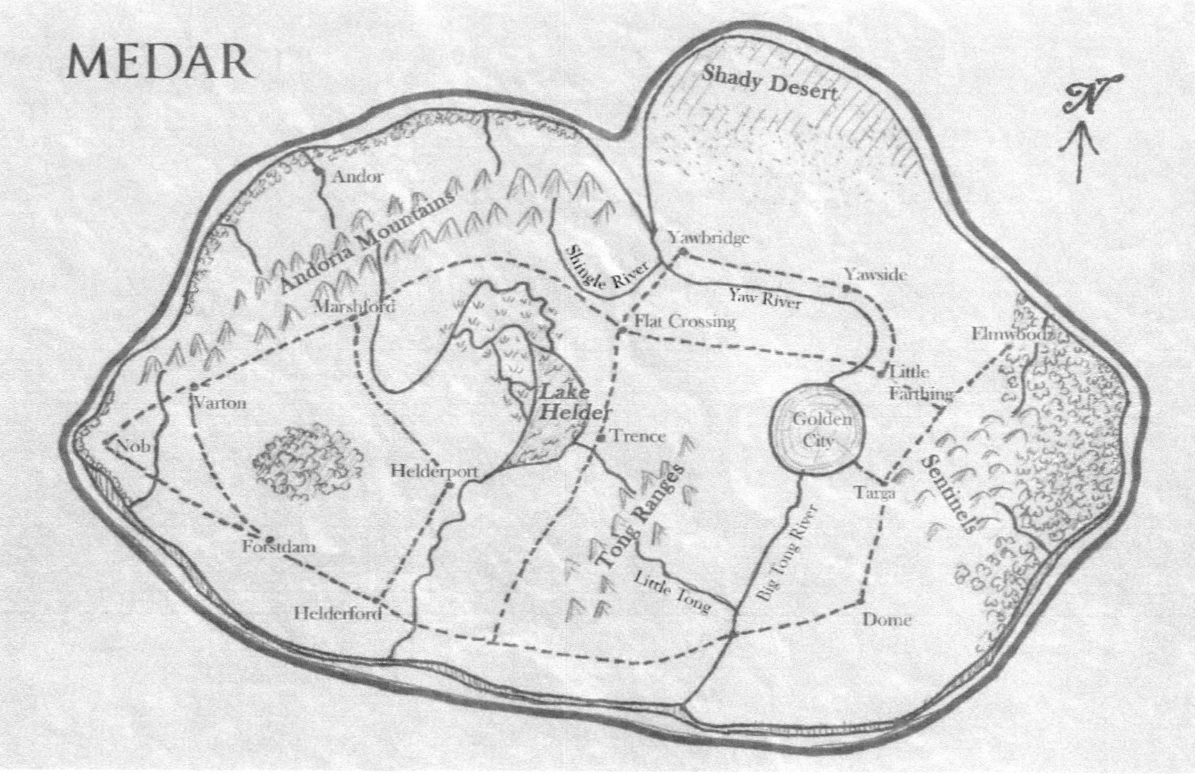

MEDAR
Shady Desert
N
Andor
Andoria Mountains
Marshford
Shingle River
Yawbridge
Yaw River
Yawside
Flat Crossing
Elmwood
Little Farthing
Varton
Lake Helder
Golden City
Nob
Trence
Tong Ranges
Targa
Sentinels
Helderport
Little Tong
Big Tong River
Forstdam
Helderford
Dome

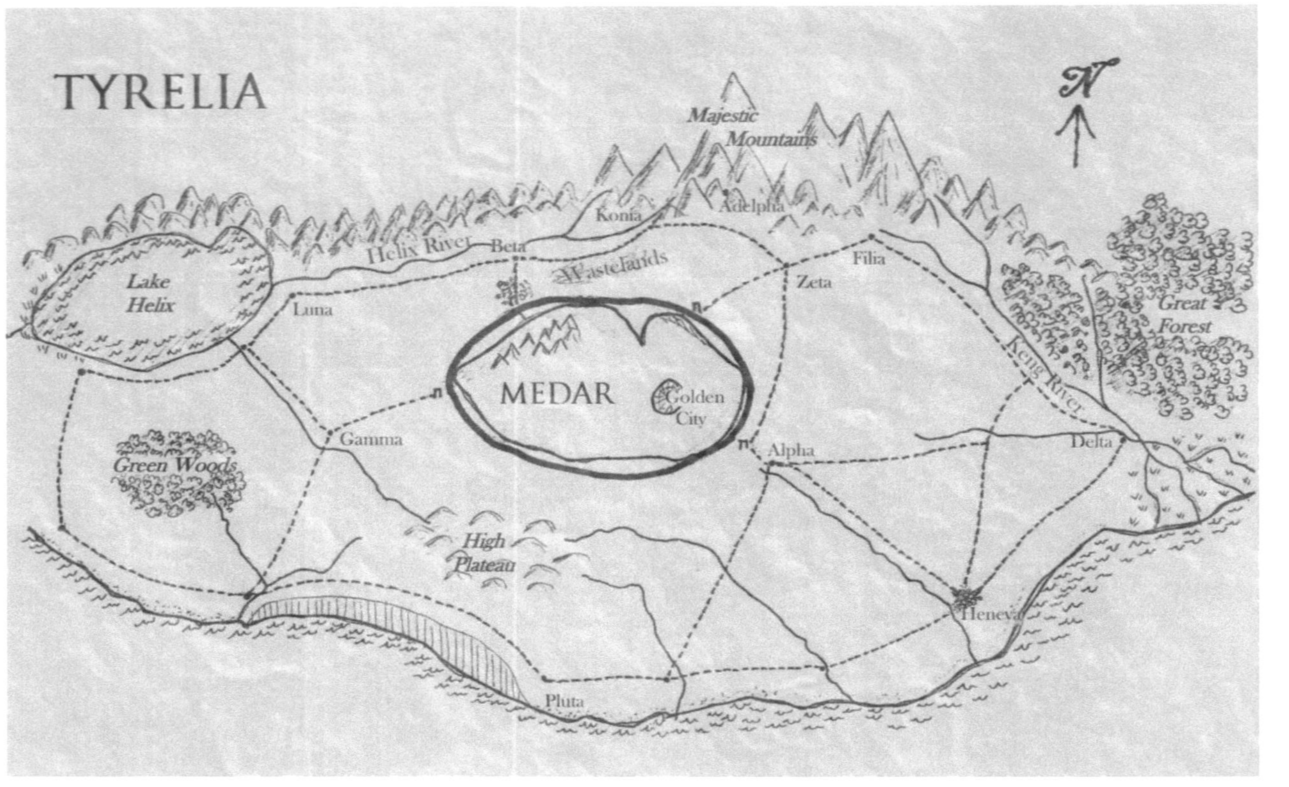

TYRELIA
N
Majestic Mountains
Konia
Adelpha
Lake Helix
Helix River
Beta
Wastelands
Zeta
Filia
Great Forest
Luna
MEDAR
Golden City
Keng River
Green Woods
Gamma
Alpha
Delta
High Plateau
Heneva
Pluta

GOLDEN CITY

Level Seven - Acedia
Level Six - Gula
Level Five - Luxuria
Level Four - Ira
Level Three - Avaritia
Level Two - Superbia
Level One - Invidia

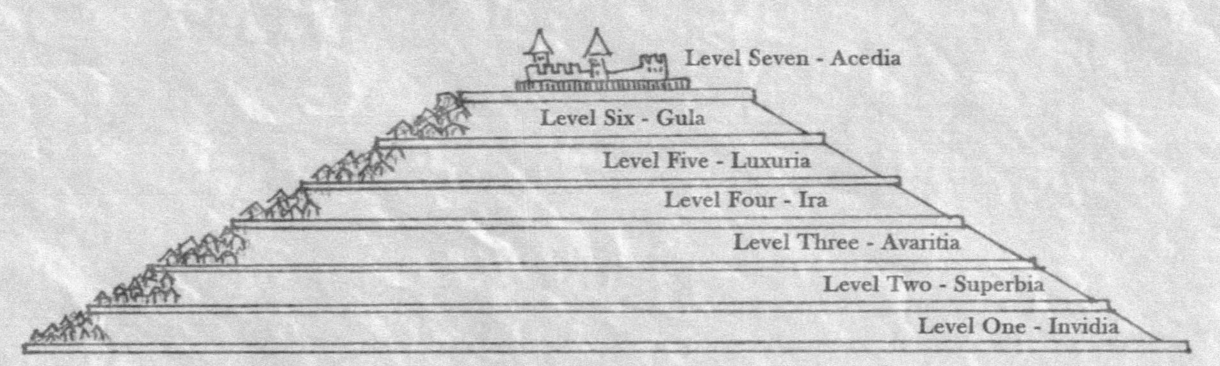

Table of Contents

Chapter 1

THE ARMOUR OF TYRELIA

Freya's heart thudded. This was it. The moment she'd been waiting for. She turned in her saddle and gazed at the army spread across the plain: immediately behind her the cavalry, mounted on their steeds, the weak sun glinting off their polished armour. Behind them the infantry waited—the archers with their bows at the ready, quivers of arrows slung on their backs; the foot soldiers armed with spear and sword. All clad in shiny breastplates, helmets, and greaves.

Freya herself wore the Armour of Tyrelia: the helmet, breastplate, and shoes. The studded shield she'd received upon entering Tyrelia nestled snugly against her back and the sword was strapped at her waist with the belt. The silver was burnished to a sheen.

Was she up to the task? She bit her lip. These people believed in her. She turned back to face the target of their attack, the seven-tiered Golden City. Unsheathing her sword in a single fluid motion, she raised it overhead. She took a deep breath and called out their enemy.

"Master of the Golden City! In the name of the Ancient, who rules Tyrelia, let the citizens go."

As her words died out, an eerie silence descended, as though the Land itself was holding its breath. Then from the heart of the City issued a deep rumbling. It swelled and swelled, until the air around them throbbed with the mocking laughter of the Master. *You?* it seemed to say. *But you're only a girl.*

It was true. She *was* only fourteen. But that hadn't stopped her unlocking the mystery of the Tablet to find the long-lost path to Tyrelia. Along the way, she'd been helped by the Watchers with their gift of invisibility and discovered that she was the subject of a one-thousand-year-old prophecy. Then, when it turned out that she was the only one who could get through the Wall, she'd entered Tyrelia alone and followed new clues to find the hermit. She lifted her chin in defiance. Let the Master underestimate her.

At that moment, a single flaming arrow shot from the topmost turret of the City. She watched it, transfixed, as it traced a smoky arc towards her. Closer and closer. She wanted to run, but she was frozen. It was heading straight for her. *Do something. Move!*

Noooo! It pierced her chest. She screamed. Clutching the arrow, she toppled in slow-motion from her horse and tumbled to the ground.

Freya woke with a start, her heart hammering. Her sheets were tangled about her legs and a clammy sweat dotted her brow. It was just a nightmare. She lay still, forcing her breathing to slow. Gradually, she calmed down. Her sight adjusted to the dimness and she glanced across the room to her friend, Willow. She was fast asleep. Tucking her long brown hair behind her ears, Freya massaged her temples, her fingers brushing against her scarred face. She'd lost one eye in a childhood accident. In Medar, she'd been teased about it and, as a result, had never had any friends … until that fateful day, almost three months ago, when, after finding the Tablet, she'd met the Watchers. For them, Freya only having one eye had been proof that she was the subject of a thousand-year-old prophecy, about *One who is not blind, but cannot see.* The Watchers had aided her every step of the way, helping her to unlock the clues in the Tablet. But they hadn't been able to help once she had reached the Wall. She'd been so scared and lonely. For five long days, she'd seen nobody and wondered if Tyrelia was abandoned. But finally, she'd arrived at the town Beta and met Willow. Here, nobody looked twice at her ruined face. It simply didn't seem to matter. She pushed her sheets aside and crawled out of her bed. Quietly, she padded out of their room and down to the main atrium of the Temple of the Adelphi.

The marble floor was cool underfoot, its solidity reassuring. A shaft of moonlight filtered through a window high above the closed doorway to illuminate the poem she'd come to read. It was engraved in large letters on the wall, opposite the door:

THE ARMOUR OF TYRELIA

Who is One who dares to believe
That if they ask, they will receive?
Who has a faith, strong and stout,
That they believe, when others doubt?
Such a One deserves to wield
The sign of faith: the studded shield

Who is One who obeys the Rules?
Who follows the Ancient when he calls?
Who has pledged to play their part,
Come what may, with all their heart?

The proof that this One serves the Realm
Is the gift of the Silver Helm

Who is One who has learned to hear
The voice of the Ancient in the air?
Who is willing to sacrifice time
To study the Ancient, learn his mind?
Such a One shall receive the reward
For their diligence, which is the Sword

Who is One who is honest and true?
Who has integrity in all they do?
Who does not play false, when they profess
Their 'no' is their 'no'; their 'yes' is their 'yes'.
Such a One, when lies are dealt
Shall receive the gift of the Belt

Who is One who knows what's right?
Who, against all odds, will stand and fight?
When others declare there's nothing wrong,
They'll stick to their beliefs; stay strong
Such a One, we celebrate
And give the gift of the Breastplate

Who is willing to go with their brothers?
To share the message of freedom with others?
To tell how the Ancient sheds his tears
For those who are lost and trapped by their fears?
Such a One, we will choose
To earn the gift of the Readiness Shoes

To such a One, despite their years,
The Tyrelian Armour shall be theirs

On the floor below the poem lay the two pieces of Armour that

Freya had already magically received. First had been the studded shield: it had simply appeared on her back within moments of her entering Tyrelia almost a month ago. At the time, she'd taken it off and tried to leave it behind but, every day, there it was, slung at her back once more. And just as well, because for her whole first week in Tyrelia, it had been the only sign that she was meant to be here. It had given her the courage to persevere.

The second piece had been the helmet. It had appeared on her head just two days ago—the day that she and Willow had finally, after three long weeks, solved the last of the clues and found the hermit. The old man had been waiting for them in his secret cave, and even knew their names. But that wasn't all: it turned out that he was the leader of the Order of the Adelphi and his name was Brother Nyx.

When Brother Nyx had first seen the shield, he'd hinted that he might know where it came from. But once the helmet, too, had magically appeared, he was certain.

"Come, come my children," he had urged in his wheezy voice. He shuffled to the cave entrance and stood surveying the green valley nestled far beneath them within the ring of mountains. A flash of silver betrayed the presence of a river, which flowed through the forest before disappearing via a fissure in the cliffs. "I need to show you something. In the Temple in Adelpha." He pointed his bony finger at the forest.

"Adelpha?" Willow asked, wonder in her voice. "That place is a myth … isn't it?"

Nyx shook his bald head, sadness in his eyes. "No. It's real. But it may as well be a myth. Nobody's lived there since the last of the Adelphi left." He sighed. Then craned his neck to look Freya in the eye. "But now that we have two novice Adelphi," he chirped, his eyes twinkling, "it shall be empty no longer. Look. There's the path. Follow that down. I'll meet you at the bottom." He indicated a track zig-zagging down the cliff face. It was narrow and steep.

"How are you getting there?" Freya asked. But there was no response. The hermit had vanished before their eyes.

Willow grunted. "He could've taken us, too."

"Well, he didn't," Freya said, "so we'd better start walking."

It took them an hour to pick their way carefully down the path, hugging the cliff face and clutching at the sparse vegetation when loose stones clattered away underfoot. At the base, they followed the trail into the forest. Shortly, they had come to a building. And not just any old building. This was the Temple. Constructed entirely of solid slabs of white marble, a peaked roof was supported by four massive columns to form a long verandah. A generous flight of stairs led up to the porch. A tall timber door was framed centrally between the two central columns. And there, in front of the door, waited the hermit, leaning on his staff.

"About time," he wheezed.

Willow shot an indignant look at Freya but, before she could complain, Nyx turned, beckoning them with his free hand.

"Come, come," he said. "Welcome to the Temple of the Adelphi." He twisted the heavy wrought-iron ring and the door swung noiselessly open.

They followed him into the cool interior. Freya had been expecting dust and cobwebs, but the place was spotless. She gazed about in wonder. Ceilings soared overhead, and smooth flagstones stretched out underfoot. Muted light filtered in through windows set high along each wall. The far wall drew her attention. Engraved words covered its entire surface. As she read it, her heart beat faster.

At her shoulder, Willow also read the words. "Oh my," she

breathed. "The Armour of Tyrelia."

Nyx shuffled closer. He bobbed his head. "Yes, yes," he said. "Your shield and helmet. They are the first two pieces of the Armour of Tyrelia."

"So," Freya said slowly, her eyes glued to the poem, "I still need to get a sword, breastplate, belt, and shoes. How am I supposed to do that?" Her voice rose as she spun to confront the hermit.

His grey eyes met her one good one. "Same as the other pieces. You earn them. Hmph."

"What do you mean 'earn them'? I didn't earn the others. They just appeared on me."

"Same thing." Nyx shrugged awkwardly, hunched over as he was. He raised a gnarled finger to point high up the wall. "Look at the first stanza. About the shield. You believed in the Ancient, even when everyone else was telling you that he wasn't real, or that he'd probably already died. That's why the shield appeared on your back the minute you stepped into Tyrelia. The first outsider for a thousand years to do so, by the way."

Freya pursed her lips. "I suppose so." The poems revealed by the Tablet had described the Ancient as the 'true and just' ruler of Tyrelia. But because nobody in Medar had ever heard of Tyrelia, let alone the Ancient, nobody had believed he existed. Except her.

Nyx nodded vigorously. "Yes. And then the second one, about the helm. What do you think caused you to earn that piece?" He peered at her from under his bushy eyebrows, now pointing at the helmet on her head.

Willow nodded slowly. "It was right after you took your vows to follow the Rules, then drank the water. I mean, I took the same pledge, but ... well, I'm not as good at following the

Rules as you."

"You can say that again," Freya muttered, remembering how Willow had chosen to ignore the Rule about only one person crossing the suspension bridge at a time, nearly causing Freya to plunge to her death. She cocked her head, as she continued to study the poem. "Oh. And you've already told us you're going to train us to learn how to hear the Ancient's voice, so I might get the sword next," she said, smiling.

"Heh. Yes. We'll commence your training in the morning. We will stay here at the Temple until you're ready. In the meantime, you may leave your shield and helmet there, at the base of the poem."

Freya took off the pieces of Tyrelian Armour and laid them reverently on the floor. She stepped backwards, staring at them, still in awe that she'd received them at all. She shook her head. "But I still don't understand. Why me? Why now?"

Nyx cleared his throat. "Well, it must be because there is a great need for a leader in a time of trouble. That's what happened last time."

"What?" Willow gasped. "The Armour has appeared before? I've never heard that."

Nyx lifted a shoulder. "It *was* a very long time ago. Come, let's sit down and I'll tell you the story." He led them into a smaller rectangular room. A long wooden trestle table ran the length. A dining hall. The hermit groaned as he sank onto a bench. "Let's eat." He reached out and rang a small bell on the table.

Within seconds, a plump woman bustled through the doorway at the other end of the room. "Brother Nyx," she exclaimed. "You're back." She stopped suddenly, staring at the girls. "Oh my. And you've brought company. Who, may I ask …?"

Nyx cleared his throat. "Hilda, may I present my new acolytes, Freya and Willow. They are the ones I told you about."

Hilda's eyebrows shot up and disappeared under the abundance of light-coloured frizzy hair that framed her ruddy face. "They're so young," she blurted.

Nyx smiled. "Yes, especially compared with this old man. But they're also quite hungry. Do you think you can rustle us up some supper? Oh, and they'll need a room prepared. Thank you, Hilda."

"Yes, of course, Sir." Hilda bobbed a curtsey and returned to the kitchen.

"I thought you said this place was empty," Willow said.

"Hmmm. Yes, empty of Adelphi, I meant. You don't expect that I'd be able to keep this place clean by myself, do you? Preposterous." Nyx chuckled. "Now, sit, sit."

Willow and Freya slid onto the bench opposite him. Patches of sunlight played on the table.

Nyx cleared his throat. "Hundreds of years before the Master built his Wall, he attempted to enter Tyrelia. *That* was a big mistake. He should've known the Ancient would never allow him to set foot in Tyrelia. So, he sent in his army instead. Those were dark times." He shook his head sadly. "Many, many Tyrelians were captured and taken to Medar. This displeased the Ancient, and he raised up a warrior by equipping him with the Armour of Tyrelia. That warrior also thought he was unworthy to receive the Armour."

"Why?" Freya asked.

"He was eighty years old, for starters. And a cripple."

"Why would the Ancient choose him, then?" Willow asked.

Nyx shook his head. "Heh, haven't you understood yet, young lady? The Ancient cares more about the condition of your heart than anything else." He stabbed his finger towards Willow's chest. "If someone is fit and healthy, but does not have a willing heart, then the Ancient won't force them to help. He seeks people to help him who will choose the greater good over their own desires."

"So, what happened?" Freya asked.

"Once he'd earned all the pieces of Armour, he rallied the Adelphi, and an army, marched into Medar and rescued the people."

"Wow, just like that?" Freya sighed. "It sounds so easy."

"No, it wasn't easy. Many people lost their lives. Some people couldn't be found. But all in all, it was a successful outcome."

Freya pressed her mouth into a line. "I hope we have a successful outcome," she said in a small voice.

Nyx beamed at her. "Of course we will. We've got the Ancient on our side. We can't lose."

~

In the dark, Freya knelt on the cool marble floor and brushed her fingers over the studs on the shield, then trailed them over the smooth surface of the silver helm. She chewed her lip. It still astonished her that she was here, in the Temple of the Adelphi, with two of the pieces of the Armour of Tyrelia that *she* had earned. She still had so many more pieces to earn and much to learn before she'd be attempting to rescue her family from the Golden City. Surely her nightmare wouldn't come true? Would she be killed by an arrow? Would she fail?

What had Brother Nyx said? That the Ancient had chosen her. It didn't seem likely that the Ancient would make a mistake and choose the wrong person. She sighed, then stood and padded back to her room. Stifling a yawn, she slipped back under her covers.

Chapter 2

TALKING STONES

Freya woke like bubbles rising to the surface. One minute she was drifting comfortably, then *pop* she burst into consciousness. Where was she? Freya shoved herself upright, scanning the room. Soaring marble ceiling. Morning sunlight filtering in through a high window. Solid oak door. Someone else sleeping on a cot on the other side of the room. Then everything fell into place. Willow. The hermit in the cave. The Temple of the Adelphi. She frowned momentarily as she recalled her dream. Nightmare more like it.

Then she smiled. This was it. Today was the day. Pushing her covers aside, she swung her legs out of the low bed and curled her toes against the cold floor. She brushed her long fringe out of her eye as she leaned towards her friend.

"Willow," she called softly. "Are you awake?"

Willow groaned and flopped an arm across her face. "No," she mumbled.

Freya crossed to her friend's bed and gently shook her shoulder. "Hey, sleepyhead … or should I say, *Adelphi?*"

Willow's eyes popped open. "Oh yeah." She grinned. "That's right." She sat up so suddenly that Freya stumbled backwards, sitting down with a thump on her bed. "What are you lazing around for?" Willow winked at Freya as she leapt out of bed and pulled her trousers on. "Race you to breakfast."

Freya squawked. Hastily pulling her own clothes on, she followed Willow to the dining hall.

Brother Nyx glanced up from his bowl of steaming porridge. "Good morning Freya, Willow. How did you sleep?"

"Good," Willow said.

"Alright," Freya said.

Nyx's bushy eyebrows drew together as he peered at her. "Just 'alright'? Is something the matter?"

"Oh, no," Freya said hastily. Maybe Brother Nyx would decide she was unworthy if she told him about her dream. "I'm good, too."

"Heh," he said. "We'll start your training straight after you've eaten."

Fifteen minutes later, they were done eating. Nyx groaned as he pushed himself up off the bench and, clutching his staff, shuffled off down a corridor, past the main atrium with the poem about the Armour of Tyrelia, right down to the end. He paused to lean his staff against the wall, before lighting a torch. The flame guttered, then took. Transferring the torch to his other hand, he gripped his staff and started down a curved flight of stairs. Freya and Willow followed slowly. Their descent was punctuated by groans and puffing from Nyx. Finally, he stopped. "Here we are," he announced, a trace of triumph in his voice.

"And where's that, then?" Willow asked from behind Freya.

Nyx coughed. "This, my young acolytes, is the vault. Hold this torch." He thrust it into Freya's hand.

A clank was followed by scraping and Freya sensed more than saw the hermit enter a room. The flame flickered, and light filled the space as she followed. She gazed about. The room was small. Four tables in the centre drew her attention. She moved towards them and gasped. Beside her Willow did the same. No, not tables, display cabinets. Peering into one of the box-like structures, her eye widened at the glittering stones arrayed upon a soft black fabric: green, blue, clear, pink ... the colours shot through with milky veins and about the size of quail eggs. She went to the next cabinet. More stones, more colours. She counted sixteen in all. She caught the hermit's eye. "Are they ...?"

The hermit nodded, his eyes crinkling at the corners. "Yes," he confirmed. "Talking stones. All that remain in Tyrelia. Apart from mine and yours, of course."

Freya's fingers curled around her stone nestled within the small leather pouch at her neck. The Cavewoman, Goh, had made the pouch for her as a parting gift, having nursed Freya back to health, many months ago.

"There are so many," Freya said.

Nyx shook his head. "Not as many as there should be. We know of at least three that are lost to us forever."

Freya winced. "You mean Paz's and Merald's stones," she said sadly, thinking of the two Watchers who had, each in their own way, given their lives for her.

"Hmmm," the hermit agreed, "but also Peri's. At least none of them have fallen into the Master's hands. *That* would be a disaster."

Willow circled the cabinets, inspecting the stones. "Can I touch them?" she asked.

Nyx bobbed his head. "Actually, you can do more than touch them. You can choose one."

Willow's head snapped up. Her eyes gleamed in the dark, reflecting the sparkle of the stones. Freya caught a flash of white teeth. "Really?" she moaned. "I can't decide."

"Well, in that case, can I make a suggestion?" the hermit offered.

Willow nodded quickly.

Nyx moved to one of the cabinets and pointed at a bright green stone. "This is wiluite."

"Oh," Willow breathed. "Just like my name. The same colour as my eyes, too. It's perfect." Her smile widened and she carefully picked up the stone.

"What are the other stones?" Freya asked.

Nyx flicked a finger as he reeled off the names. "Well, let's see, we've got jade, fire agate, garnet, turquoise, alexandrite—"

Willow twitched at this one.

"—diamond, quartz, zircon, opal, beryl, amber, pearl, jasper, tanzanite and moonstone."

"Freya, have you noticed the relationship between a stone and its bearer?" Nyx asked, peering at her intently.

"What, you mean the colour? Willow's just chosen a stone the same colour as her eyes, but mine's multi-coloured and yours is black. They hardly match our eyes."

Brother Nyx stroked his chin. "I meant more the relationship between the stone's colour and its bearer's name. Think of your father Rube's stone."

"It's red," Freya squeaked. "Ruby-red."

The hermit nodded, smiling.

"And Saff's stone is blue—that's sapphire, isn't it?" Freya said.

"Yes," Nyx replied, "and I'm guessing the stone you inherited from Merald was emerald-green?"

Freya nodded enthusiastically. Then she paused, frowning. "What would Thyst's one be? I never saw her use it."

"That would be amethyst. Purple."

Willow huffed. "Hold on a moment." She faced a palm outward as if to stop the conversation. "So, you're telling us that all these people, these Adelphi or Watchers, just happened to be born with names that matched the colour of one of these talking stones here?" Her voice rose, her expression incredulous.

Nyx barked a short laugh. "What a ridiculous notion. Of course not. It's part of the ceremony when they become an Adelphi. They select their stone and choose a name to suit."

A tingle ran down Freya's spine. "It's like a secret identity." A thought struck her. "What's my stone?" She extracted it from the pouch at her throat. The multi-coloured stone glittered.

"It's fluorite, but …"

"But what?"

"I think it's close enough to your name that we don't need to change it. If you agree."

Freya grinned and tucked her stone away. "Agreed."

Willow's expression cleared. "That makes more sense. You know, I'd been wondering how come your name was the same as the Leader of the Adelphi you told us about in the cave: the one who retrieved these stones after the Master's Wall went up. I thought maybe … you were a thousand years old. I'm such an idiot." The last part came out in a rush.

Nyx patted Willow's arm. "No, you're no idiot, my dear. My stone is onyx, and it is tradition that every Leader of the Adelphi takes the name Nyx." He sighed. "I was almost beginning to think that I would be the very last Nyx." His face brightened. "But then you two came along, just as foreseen, and here we are. Now. Let's practise using the stones. Back upstairs, please."

~

Freya sat cross-legged on a woven mat on the floor of the hermit's cave, high above the forest canopy that concealed the Temple of the Adelphi in the valley. It had been quite a climb. She squinted, concentrating her thoughts on the multi-hued talking stone nestled in her upturned palm. Suddenly, the stone glowed and grew warm. A whitish halo the size of a melon, shot through with all the colours of the rainbow, formed around it. The colours shifted and pulsed, intensifying in some areas while in others they disappeared altogether, until they settled into the image of Willow's face.

"Hi Willow," Freya said.

The ghostly image swirling above her palm looked surprised. "Wow," said Willow. "This is cool. I can really hear you. Like you're right beside me."

Freya had been using talking stones for a few months now and was familiar with the process of focussing her thoughts on the person she wanted to talk to, but this was Willow's first time. Freya grinned. "I know, right? Do you want to try calling me now?"

"Sure."

Freya closed her fist around the stone to cut off the communication, then opened it again. Not wanting to influence Willow's attempt to create the connection, she studied the cave—looking anywhere but at her stone. She examined a rudimentary painting on the cave wall: two seated human shapes holding something in front of them, surrounded by bits of green and blue. Huh? That was strange. Although she'd only glimpsed it when she and Willow had first entered this cave, she was certain there had only been one figure in the painting before. And hadn't the figure been standing?

Just then, the stone in her palm warmed and glowed. Sure enough, the multi-coloured haze formed into Willow's grinning face. "I did it," she crowed.

"You sure did," Freya said.

"Brother Nyx says he's going to come and get you now," Willow said, after glancing to the side. "He said to make sure you're up against the wall."

Freya scrambled to her feet and pressed herself against the painting. Within moments, Nyx appeared in the middle of the cave.

Freya yelped. "You … did that appearing thing."

"Mmm," the hermit agreed. "It's called warping. Are you ready to leave, my child? Come."

As soon as he gripped her arm, a buzzing filled her ears and her skin tingled with vibrations. She squeezed her eyes shut as the humming and throbbing engulfed her. She was falling. She screamed and flung her other arm out. It all stopped as suddenly as it had started. She stumbled to the ground at the foot of the Law Pillar adjacent to the Temple, Nyx still gripping her arm.

She panted heavily. "I feel sick," she moaned. The only other time she had warped had been by accident and that time she'd blacked out.

Nyx leaned on his staff. "You're doing well. You're a natural. Come along now. Willow will be wondering where we've got to."

Freya climbed slowly to her feet and followed the old man inside.

Chapter 3

THE BRIDGE RE-BUILD

Watcher Saff peered over the cliff edge. Far below, about twenty of the diminutive Cave People toiled to repair the broken bridge that used to span the Chasm—a stomach-churning drop that surrounded Medar, completely separating it from Tyrelia.

Saff and Watcher Thyst had arrived seven days ago. Freya had stumbled across the Cave People when she'd first escaped her death sentence after being denied entry to the Golden City all those months ago. Well, more like she'd collapsed near where Saff was standing now, and the Cave People had taken her in. When he and Thyst had discovered they couldn't accompany Freya into Tyrelia, because the Wall was blocking their way, they'd had to find somewhere safe to go. So, they'd followed Freya's directions and here they were, with the Cave People.

But they didn't speak the language. The Cave People spoke in guttural grunts and clicks. Saff and Thyst had learned a few words, but mostly they used signs and hand gestures. It was amazing how much you could communicate without words.

Saff had managed to convey what needed to be done to

rebuild the twenty-metre-long section of missing bridge. And because of their friendship with Freya, the Cave People had agreed to help. Below him, in the cave network, dozens of women had been busy weaving vine fibres into strong ropes. Behind him, the men had selected the straightest, tallest trees and felled them using primitive axes. A noisy exercise, but fortunately they were far from the Golden City. The closest town was Targa, but there we no roads through the Sentinel Hills or the neighbouring forest to where these caves lay hidden. Saff was sure the Master was unaware of the existence of the Cave People. Really, it had been a stroke of luck that Freya had found them in the first place.

Under Saff's supervision, the Cave People lashed the trunks together with the ropes, one trunk offset half-way up its neighbour, such that two rows comprising five trunks each achieved the desired length. Now, slowly, slowly, a group of men lowered the bound section into the Chasm. They grunted with exertion, sweat beading their brows as they strained against the weight.

Saff leaned over the edge. Even though he knew they didn't understand him, he couldn't help himself. "Steady, steady," he cautioned. "Watch out below!"

Five men grabbed the dangling base of the logs and manoeuvred them into position near the broken edge of the bridge. Then they busied themselves securing the ends of the timbers to the existing bridge section. The women had spent days fashioning a woven sleeve to receive the new logs. After guiding the base of the trees snugly into the casing, they fed another length of rope in and around and around, binding the logs to the sleeve.

Saff nodded with satisfaction, fingering his black beard. So far so good. Time to test it, then. He turned to the men next to him, still holding the rope taut to prevent the logs slipping sideways, and motioned, as if pushing something away from his body, pointing down into the Chasm.

The man closest to the cliff edge nodded in understanding. Releasing the rope, he crouched and called to another group of men positioned in a cave, about halfway down the rock face. The man issued some commands, gesticulating. The men in the lower cave picked up a long bamboo pole and set the notched end against the lashed tree trunks protruding above the lip of their cave. As they pushed the trunks away from the cliff with the pole, the men up above eased the rope tension. Slowly, the entire structure tilted further and further away into the Chasm, pivoting on its fixed base.

Saff switched his gaze from the rope at the top to the distance it needed to travel. Had they made the rope long enough? Would the small men be strong enough to control it?

He chewed his nails, following the slow progress of the trees. They stopped moving. The men beside made agitated noises. "What's wrong?" he asked. But he needn't have, as he understood immediately: the pole was too short to push the trees any further.

The leader issued some barked instructions. The men in the cave below picked up the bamboo pole and hurried down the stairs hewn into the cliff face. A few minutes later they appeared at the mouth of an even lower cave. Once more, they eased the pole out towards the trees. It circled a few times before connecting with its intended target. They continued pushing outwards.

Now the structure was vertical. Saff held his breath. This was it. The men with the pole gave the trees a slight nudge. The trees remained upright. With a shout, the Cave People thrust the pole out once more and slowly, slowly, the trees tilted away. Cheers and clapping erupted. The men adjacent to Saff shouted. He tore his gaze away from the action below. The men strained against the rope. More jumped to their aid, adding their strength to the task. The trees were falling too fast.

Saff hitched up his robes, ran to the back of the line and grabbed the rope. It slipped through his hands. He gripped harder, his knuckles white. His eyes watered. He grunted and, bracing himself against the ground, wrapped the rope around his forearms before throwing his weight backwards. The rope stopped moving. Breathing heavily, he strained to release a section of the rope. When he saw that the men in front of him had gained control, he wrapped it around his waist and slowly fed it forward. A steady rhythm developed. A bead of sweat dripped into his eye. He blinked rapidly but daren't let go of the rope to wipe it off. He flicked his head. Suddenly, a cheer went up. At the same moment, he realised that the weight had come off the rope. They'd done it!

He unwrapped himself and followed the others down the stairs, mopping his face with his sleeve. Down, down he jogged. Past caves, under the waterfall and finally to the landing where the bridge began.

A crowd had gathered already, but it parted as the people saw Saff. Joining his palms together in front of his chest in the gesture he'd learned to thank them, he moved eagerly to the front. He surveyed their handiwork. He smiled. It had worked. The bound pairs of trunks spanned the gap. Of course, this was only the first piece. They'd need to repeat the whole exercise another three times. Still, it was a start.

His eyes travelled the length of the new span and up the cliff face opposite, following the faint zig-zag lines of the staircase. They were too deep within the Chasm to see it, but at the top, Tyrelia awaited them. *If* they could get through the Wall. He pursed his lips. Freya had been the first. When they'd finally reached the Chasm on the other side of the Andoria Mountains, Guards hot in pursuit, she'd seen Tyrelia. Just like that. He shook his head in amazement at the memory. The Wall had gone, she'd claimed. When they'd finally found the long-lost bridge, far from here, and climbed up the other side, Freya had stepped straight into Tyrelia. But for Thyst and himself, the Wall was as solid and impenetrable as it had ever been. They were unable to enter.

Thyst had been next. Nearly two weeks ago, on their way to the Cave People, she discovered that the Wall had disappeared for her, too. Rube had suspected the reason, and Brother Nyx had confirmed it: it was a wall of unbelief. Unbelief in the Ancient, who ruled Tyrelia. It had been a relief when they'd finally re-established their connection with Freya. It had been worrying not hearing from her for so long, but finally, just two days ago, she'd contacted him. Turned out she'd broken her stone. Despite that, she'd persevered. The Tablet had revealed new messages that had led her to the hermit, Brother Nyx. She'd told them that everyone in Tyrelia believed in the Ancient, although no one had actually *met* him. She'd taken some sort of vow that made her a citizen of Tyrelia and now she was training to become an Adelphi—like him. That girl had real belief, no doubt about it. Maybe the Ancient really did exist?

A shout startled him from his reverie. The Cave People yelled and raced up the stairs. What was going on? He followed them, scanning over their heads for clues to the commotion.

"Saff." Thyst's voice cut through the clamour. She stood in the mouth of a cave ahead, gesticulating wildly, her purple robes flapping. Her brown curls bounced around her face, her violet eyes wide.

"What is it? What's happened?" Saff panted when he reached her.

"Guards! The Master's Guards. They're here." Thyst pointed above her head. "Come on, let's go."

Saff sprinted up the stairs behind her. Even before they reached the top, Thyst had nocked an arrow to her bow. Saff scrambled over the lip of the cliff, hot on Thyst's heels. Cavemen and Guards disappeared into the forest ahead. He turned himself invisible and followed them in. He jumped over a dead Guard and set another in his sights. But before he reached him, the Guard toppled, an arrow protruding from his chest. Saff recognised it as one of Thyst's.

There! Another one. He zig-zagged around the trees, chasing his quarry. This time, two small figures took the Guard down. He hadn't even seen them until they leaped. They swiftly sliced the Guard's neck, killing him cleanly. Saff stopped and scanned the woods. No Guards. He allowed himself to become visible again and leaned on his sword, breathing heavily.

He spotted Thyst. "Nice shot," he called.

She smiled. "Thanks. Saff, did you notice that these Guards look a bit different?"

"What? No. What do you mean?" Saff strode over to one lying nearby. "Oh, yes, I see. They look sort of … rotten. Look how grey and slack his skin is."

Thyst's eyes widened. "Rotten, you say?"

Saff stroked his beard, staring at the dead Guard. "Are they a different race, do you think?"

Thyst shook her head. "Freya said that once. That the Guards looked rotten."

Saff whipped his head up, his blue eyes narrowed. "Really?

When?"

"At the crest of the pass over the Andoria Mountains. Right before she discovered that the Wall was gone, and she could see Tyrelia."

Saff sucked his breath in, then turned and ran towards the Chasm. As soon as he cleared the forest, he stopped in his tracks, staring.

Thyst ran to him. She studied his face and smiled. "You can see it."

Saff beamed and spun to hug her. He let her go and gazed back across the Chasm. "Yes," he breathed. "At last, I can see Tyrelia."

Beside him, Thyst nodded. "And you know what that means?"

Saff glanced at her. She had beautiful eyes. He'd never noticed them being so stunning before. Maybe seeing Tyrelia was affecting him. "No, what does it mean?"

"It means you believe in the Ancient," she said.

He smiled back at her. She had a very pretty smile, too. They locked eyes. His heart started beating triple time. Unthinking, his hand cupped her cheek. Her skin was so smooth. "Thyst," he said, "you're beautiful. I …"

Then her lips were on his. Soft. He gathered her into his arms. She fit perfectly.

They were interrupted by one of the Cavemen, a huntsman, tugging on Saff's sleeve, tearing them apart.

"What's wrong?" he asked.

The man gestured wildly towards the Chasm then tugged harder, drawing Saff forward.

"Okay, we're coming," Saff said laughing, pulling a face at Thyst.

She smiled and squeezed his arm. "We'd better go see what

this is about."

They followed him down the cliff face into the large meeting cave. Packed, it hummed with conversation. Saff and Thyst hovered near the entrance. An expectant hush settled over the gathering. As the clan Chief entered, his wolfskin cloak flowing behind him, the crowd parted to let him and his spear-bearing guards through. The floor of the cave was higher at the rear, forming a natural stage. The Chief stepped on to it and gestured for quiet. He spoke for a short time, ending his speech with a finger in the air. A murmur of dismay rippled through the crowd. Then he left as abruptly as he'd arrived. As he passed them, Saff reached out a hand. "What's happened?" he blurted out.

One of the chief's guards thrust his spear at Saff's chest, and Saff stumbled back against the wall. The chief said something, and the guard lowered his spear, but still glared at Saff.

"One," the chief said. "One run. Understand?"

Saff nodded. His blood hammered in his ears.

Thyst slipped her hand into his. "What is it Saff? What was that about?"

Saff turned to her. "One Guard got away. We'd better call Brother Rube. Immediately."

Chapter 4

JACK'S OPPORTUNITY

Jack's mind whirled as he made his way towards the Level One Games Arena. Last night had been … interesting. He'd gone to the prison and seen his da. Da had looked terrible, after being locked up for nearly two weeks. Jack's plan had been straightforward: show the Guards where Rube was, claim the ten-thousand-unit reward for turning him in, use the money to secure the release of Da and reunite his parents. Then he wouldn't need to feel guilty about buying his way up to Level Two and leaving his ma alone. Sure, Rube had been helping them ever since they'd become trapped inside the Golden City. The Guards called him a Transient, but Rube called himself a Watcher. Whatever he was, he could turn himself invisible, and get in and out of the City. Jack had only just learned that his sister, Freya, was adopted, when Rube had found them a week after their arrival and shocked them all with the news that he was Freya's real father. Since then, Rube had been communicating with Freya and the other Watchers and trying to figure out how to break the power of the injection that trapped them inside the City. His parents and Rube thought the City was a bad place. A trap. But Jack *liked* the Golden City.

He didn't need to be freed.

Things hadn't quite gone to plan, though. He'd got to the prison all right and insisted on seeing that Da was alive before Jack informed on Rube. Then he'd led the Guards to their neighbours—Hank and Leena's—house, where he'd left Rube only an hour or so earlier. However, when they got there, Rube had gone. And not just invisible-gone. They'd made sure that there was no way anybody, even an invisible one, could've escaped their search. Rube definitely wasn't in that house. It was a mystery. Jack absent-mindedly rubbed his knuckle. Hank and Leena must've known what he was planning, and then hidden Rube somewhere else. Maybe that's why Leena had been a bit strange with him this morning. Or maybe she was just angry with him for bringing Guards in to ransack her house in the middle of the night. Either way, the Guards hadn't arrested Rube, so Jack hadn't got the reward. Simple as that. Which meant that Da was still in prison, and Jack was no closer to buying his way up to Level Two.

It had been his ambition, ever since he'd clapped eyes on the higher levels, to get to the top level of the City. Stacked one on top of the other, like layers on a wedding cake, each level better off than the one below. When they'd first moved here, he'd thought that the reason nobody ever left was because they were content with their level. Now, he knew it was because each level had its own injection which prevented people from leaving. But their house here in Level One was so much nicer than where they'd lived before, in Nob. They *were* better off, no matter what his parents thought. Weren't they? He recalled the time a man had died at his feet, trying to flee from Level Two. And that other time he'd witnessed the Master's black carriage careening through the streets. For some reason he couldn't explain, it had sent chills down his spine. He shook the thoughts out of his head, like shaking a spider out of his shoe. As long as you didn't get in the Master's way, then the City offered plenty of opportunity to progress one's situation. Provided you could afford it.

He sighed. Well, if he wasn't going to get the reward money, he'd better improve his betting skills and win some wrestling matches—and the gold that went with it. The arena was just ahead. He quickened his pace and passed through the constricting archways that controlled the flow of people. "Hi," Jack hailed Straw and Hay, his wrestling buddies.

"Hi Jack. How's your back?" Straw asked.

Instinctively, Jack rubbed his lower back. He'd strained it last week, when he not only lost his match, but also his bet on himself. Hence his decision to inform on Rube. "It's good, good. Never felt better."

"You've looked better, though," Straw commented.

Jack knew he was sporting dark rings under his eyes. "Yeah, didn't sleep so well last night. Worried about Ma and Da, you know?" He ran a hand through his dark brown hair.

Hay nodded thoughtfully. "You've had a run of bad luck lately, Jack." He glanced at his brother. "Straw and I've been thinking."

"Sounds dangerous."

Straw punched Jack gently on his arm. "Don't be rude, man, or we might not share our brilliant idea with you." He turned on his heel and strode off towards the betting tent.

Jack stared at him a second before jogging after him. "I'm not sure if you remember, but I lost all my money last week. I can't place a bet."

Hay smirked. "Yeah, we remember. That's where our brilliant plan comes in." He clamped his mouth shut.

Jack groaned. "Come on, guys. Tell me what your brilliant

minds have come up with. *Please.*"

Straw turned his head to stare haughtily at Jack.

Jack sighed. "Do enlighten me. I am your humble servant."

Straw grinned. "I'm going to remember you said that. Alright. Here's what we're going to do." He slung his arm around Jack's shoulder. Not only were Straw and Hay both taller than Jack, they were both strong and burly, being apprentice blacksmiths by trade. Jack used to be just a farmer. "Let's sit over there where it's nice and quiet." Straw jerked his head towards the bleachers that lined the oval stadium. "You know, Hay and I are smashing our division. We've checked the draw, and we reckon we can both win our matches today."

Hay nodded briefly. "We've also checked the odds," he added, shooting a glance at the betting tent. "If Straw's opponent wins, whoever bets on that stands to make quite a large amount. We'd have enough to buy our way up to Level Two."

Jack frowned. "But … won't the officials suspect there's something up if you lose?"

Straw shrugged. "Not if I do a Jack. Accidents happen."

Jack gripped the timber bleacher so hard a splinter pierced his palm. His heart filled with lead. "Oh," he said in a small voice. "That—that's great. I'm happy for you." He faced away from them, swallowing hard.

"You idiot," Straw said. "When we say 'our' we mean us three. We could *all* buy our way up together. Whaddaya think?"

The lead drained out of Jack's heart and through the soles of his feet. He grinned. "Are you serious? Do you really mean it?"

Sporting an identical grin, Hay nodded enthusiastically. His spiky white-blond hair shivered from the roots, looking for all the Land like hay blowing in the wind. "Of course we mean it.

Told you it was brilliant."

Straw clapped Jack on the back. "Let's place those bets. Then we have some wrestling to do."

~

Jack burst through his front door. His ma was sitting at the kitchen table.

Ma jumped. "Jack. You startled me. Where have you been? I went to the wrestling ring after I was done at the Guards' ale tent, but you'd left already."

Jack smiled affectionately and pulled Ma out of her chair. It was good she'd got the job of serving ale in the Guards' tent. She and Leena had been able to glean all sorts of useful information about Freya from the Guards' conversations. It had meant that she couldn't watch his games, though. He spun her around. "Well, that's because the lads and I were celebrating."

"Did you win, my love? I'm so sorry I wasn't there to see it."

"Yes, I did. But not only that, Straw and Hay won as well." He remembered just in time that he hadn't told his ma about the betting. Best to leave out the details of how they got the money.

Martha smiled fondly at him. "That's wonderful. I'm so happy for you all."

Jack hugged his ma then, placing his hands on her shoulders, looked her in the eye. "There's something else I need to tell you. We've got enough to buy our way up to Level Two. We've already arranged it with the Guards. I just need to pack up my things and we can go." He blurted it out in a rush.

A strange expression crossed his ma's features. Panic?

"Oh," she said. She sat down again. "I can't … don't want to leave Level One, Jack."

"No, Ma, I didn't mean you." Drat, that came out all wrong.

His cheeks burning, he pulled out a chair and dropped into it. He grabbed her hands. "I'm sorry, Ma. I know I'm leaving you here all alone. I really am. I tried to get Da out of prison, but it's no good. I'm just making things worse for you all. Anyway, I'm nearly nineteen now. It's time I made my own way here." His voice trailed off. How would she react? She'd been so fragile recently.

She withdrew her hand from between his and patted them. "It's okay, Jack." She lifted his chin and smiled tenderly. "Don't you worry. I'll be fine. You're right, you're a grown man now. You do need to make your own way. Come and give your ma a hug."

Jack pushed out a breath as he hugged her. She was taking this remarkably well. "Thanks, Ma. I love you. Can you … when you see Da, can you tell him I love him, too?"

Martha nodded. "Yes, of course. Now, let's get your things together. Mustn't keep those nice boys waiting."

It didn't take long to pack. He stuffed all his clothes into a small satchel. His razor and comb followed. His notebook with his wrestling notes and pencil. Lastly, his bag of coins. That was the lot.

Ma accompanied them to the Level Two gate.

Jack squinted at the inscription above the archway: *SUPERBIA*. Rube had told them that each level had a different name, but he didn't know what they meant. Jack guessed now he'd never know.

The Guard, who was to escort them, waited with arms folded. He tapped his foot, his swarthy features set in a scowl, as Jack hugged Martha, and Straw and Hay farewelled their parents.

Jack pressed a handful of coins into Martha's palm and closed her fingers around them.

"Jack, no," she protested.

He shook his head. "I'm just sorry it's not more, Ma." Then, with one last hug, he turned and followed the Guard through the small door concealed by the shadow of the archway. It was identical to the one under the Level One archway, through which they'd entered when they'd first arrived in the Golden City two months ago. A second Guard awaited them in the dim interior. At least this time Jack was expecting the injection. He rolled up his sleeve and offered his arm. As the cool liquid flowed into his veins a thought flitted into his brain. *This is it. No turning back now. I'll never leave the City again.* He glanced uncertainly at Straw and Hay and rolled his sleeve down. Hay winked at him. Straw gave him a thumbs-up. Jack smiled back. *Onwards and upwards.*

Chapter 5

LEARNING TO WARP

Freya and Willow perched on the top step of the temple stairway, listening with rapt attention to Nyx.

At the base of the stairs, Nyx leaned heavily on his staff. "Freya and Willow, you have both experienced warping. You travelled between Law Pillars. How do you think that happened?"

Freya closed her eyes, remembering. After revealing the clue in the sulphurous steam of the Wastelands, they'd come across a Law Pillar. The tall, stone structure was engraved with the four Laws of Tyrelia. It had *called* her. "First of all, when we got close enough to the pillar, there was this really weird buzzing in my ears, and the air was pulsing," she said.

"Yeah, but it wasn't *that* much more pulsing than normal," Willow objected.

"Maybe it's normal for you. But it was one of the first things I noticed when I entered Tyrelia—the vibrations. You just don't get that in Medar."

Nyx nodded. "So, Freya, you heard buzzing and sensed the vibrations. Then what happened?"

"I just sort of … walked towards the pillar. I couldn't help myself. It was like a magnet."

"Yeah," Willow interjected. "She completely ignored me. I was calling her and calling her, but it was as if she was sleep-walking."

"Then what happened?" Nyx asked.

"I grabbed Freya's arm," Willow said. "I thought maybe … I dunno, something bad was going to happen." She cut her eyes at her friend.

"I don't really remember that," Freya said, frowning. "I remember falling. The vibrations were powerful. They were thrumming in my head. Then we landed. Whump! And the humming stopped. Just like that. I sat up and I saw Willow lying there beside me. I thought—I thought she was dead."

"But I wasn't," Willow chipped in. "Even better, we were in Konia where my parents live. We'd saved ourselves a 200-rata journey."

"Why do you think you ended up in Konia, and not somewhere else?" Nyx asked.

Freya lifted a shoulder. "I have no idea. I'd never heard of it before Willow told me she was from there."

It was Willow's turn to frown. "Now that you mention it, I was thinking about getting to Konia when I grabbed your arm. Do you think …?" She looked at Nyx.

He clapped his hands, smiling. "Yes, Willow. You travel between Law Pillars on the vibrations by thinking about where you want to go. You *will* yourself to your destination."

"Wow," Freya and Willow said in unison.

"So … you can go wherever you like, then?" Freya asked.

Nyx shook his head. "Not exactly. The vibrations are … how can I put it? They're the will of the Ancient."

Freya wrinkled her brow. "The Ancient's will? How does that work?"

Nyx cleared his throat. "The whole of Tyrelia operates according to the Ancient's Rules."

Freya elbowed Willow in her side. Willow blushed.

"And the vibrations are a physical manifestation of the Ancient's will. When you *want* to follow the Ancient's Rules, you harmonise with the vibrations. Warping, or travelling on the vibrations, is one way of acting in line with what the Ancient wants. Or, put another way, of doing things that will benefit Tyrelia and all those who inhabit it."

"That makes sense," Freya said slowly. "I was following the clues in the Tablet. They were leading me to you. And going to Konia was travelling in the right direction. Does that mean …" she bit her lip, "… that I was *supposed* to find Willow, and the Ancient wanted her here, too?"

"It's not so much the Ancient particularly wanting Willow — or you, for that matter," Nyx added hurriedly, seeing Willow's scowl. "But the Ancient can use anyone who is willing to listen and to follow."

Willow cocked her head. "Hang on a minute. Earlier you said that we warp between Law Pillars. But you warped from your cave down to here, and there's no pillar in your cave."

Nyx harrumphed. "That's right. Warping between the pillars is a way to guarantee that you're not going to land on someone when you arrive. But when you're as experienced as I am, you don't need the pillars. Besides, I could see there was no one where I wanted to go. Now, are you ready to try?"

Freya glanced at Willow, unsure. She shrugged. "I suppose so."

Willow cracked her knuckles. "Right. What do we do?"

"I'll start with you, Willow, as you haven't warped recently. Come. We'll walk slowly towards the pillar, and I'll hold your elbow like this." Nyx grasped Willow's elbow. "Then I'll warp us to the capital, Heneva."

Freya watched them intently. As they neared the pillar, their outlines blurred, like they were in a mirage. Then they were gone. She gripped the step. *One, two, three,* she counted. She got up to one hundred and sixty before they came back. Willow fell to her knees, panting, her face white. The hermit, on the other hand, looked unaffected. He hobbled towards Freya.

"Are you all right?" Freya called.

Willow looked up. "Yeah. I just feel a bit shaky." She pushed herself upright and stumbled over to the steps, where she flopped back down.

"Your turn now, Freya." Nyx beckoned to her.

Freya leapt up. "Are we going to Heneva, too?"

Nyx nodded.

"What's it like?"

"You'll see."

Freya's heart thumped as she approached. Would she feel sick again? As Nyx took her elbow, the familiar thrumming vibrated through her and before she knew it, they had left the hidden green valley and were standing near another pillar. Freya stumbled slightly, but Nyx held her steady. She gulped some air. They were in a plaza, bustling with people. A gentle breeze lifted her hair off her scarred face. The air smelled of salt. Nobody paid them any heed.

"Ready to go?" Nyx whispered in her ear.

"Sure," Freya said.

The vibrations engulfed her and, in a blink, Freya was back in the valley. She took a few deep breaths but was otherwise steady on her feet.

"How was that?" Nyx asked.

"Much better," Freya replied. "But … why wasn't anyone in Heneva surprised to see us?"

Nyx chuckled. "Because we were invisible, my dear."

"I didn't realise," Freya said. "Awesome. Now what?"

"I'm going to take you each individually a few more times. We'll stay a bit longer, so you can start to familiarise yourselves with Heneva for when I send you there by yourselves."

By midday, they had visited Heneva three more times each. Freya had become used to the sensation and didn't feel so nauseous. She chattered with Willow as they slid into their seats in the dining hall for lunch.

"Did you notice their clothes?" Willow enthused. "Amazing colours. And way more outrageous than Konia or Beta."

"Mmm," Freya agreed, grabbing a slice of fresh bread and layering it with cheese and salami. "The colours." She took a big bite.

Nyx served himself some beans. "After lunch, I want you to try warping by yourselves."

Willow's mouth dropped open. "Without you?"

Nyx nodded. "Yes. Without each other, too."

"But we can't turn ourselves invisible. People will see us," Freya objected.

"I don't want you to warp to Heneva. I suggest you warp to that Law Pillar near the Wastelands. You're familiar with the location and there are unlikely to be people there."

"What if it doesn't work? I mean, what if we end up somewhere else and can't get back?"

Nyx chuckled. "Well, just call me and I'll come and get you."

Willow slapped the table. "Of course. Using our talking stones. This Adelphi stuff is *so* cool. I wish Alex could be here." She sighed.

Freya agreed. They had last seen Willow's twin brother when he had helped them with the final clue, to find the crevice that led them to the hermit's cave and this secret valley. Alex had a wicked sense of humour—like Willow. Sometimes their mischief went a bit too far, but the twins were both so much fun, you couldn't help but like them. She wouldn't mind him being with them, either. He was kind of cute, and he seemed to like her, too. Her thoughts drifted to her own brother, Jack. He was so much older than her, so they hadn't been close like Willow and Alex. But she still missed him.

When they'd eaten, Freya and Willow headed back out to the pillar. "You can go first, if you like," Freya offered.

"Thanks." Willow approached the structure, her hands twitching at her sides. She glanced back at Freya, who gave her a thumbs-up. Willow hesitated, scrutinising the pillar.

What was she waiting for? "You can do it," Freya called out.

"I'm trying, and I don't think I can." Willow faced the column once more, her fists clenched. Then she spun and ran back to Freya. She threw herself down on the steps. "Your turn," she mumbled.

Freya felt the vibrations before she heard them. *The pillar by the Wastelands.* She pictured it in her mind. And then she was there! She sniffed the familiar sulphurous fumes. Time to go back. She allowed the pulsing air to engulf her, visualising the pillar next to the Temple of the Adelphi. In a heartbeat, she was back. Willow was still moping on the temple steps. As Freya moved towards her, trying to figure out what to say, she realised that she was holding something. She stopped and looked down at her hand. *A sword. By the Ancient.*

Willow leaped off the steps. "Freya's got the sword," she yelled. "Brother Nyx, Brother Nyx!" She ran to Freya and gave her a big hug. "You did it," she exclaimed, grinning.

Freya drew the blade from its leather scabbard and lifted it to inspect it with her single eye. Intricately engraved its entire length, the silver blade glinted in the sunlight. A plain guard separated the blade from the leather-wrapped hilt. She didn't know anything about swords but, somehow, she expected it to be heavier. She looked at Willow in wonder.

Willow reached out a hand. "Can I hold it?" she asked.

"Sure." Freya handed it over.

Willow swished it through the air, slicing first one way then the other. "Very nice," she said.

"Have you used a sword before?" Freya asked.

Willow peered down her nose at Freya. "Of course … not," she laughed.

Willow was such a clown. Freya was still giggling when Nyx arrived.

"Well done, Freya," he panted as he hobbled over. "You are *One who has learned to hear the voice of the Ancient in the air*," he quoted.

Freya's cheeks grew warm. "I didn't really do anything special," she mumbled.

"Yes, you did," Willow admonished. "Look at me. I couldn't even leave the valley. You not only left and came back, you came back with a sword."

"Let's put it with the other pieces," Nyx said. As they made their way inside, he asked Willow, "Did I hear you say that you weren't able to warp anywhere?"

Willow fiddled with her collar. "Maybe," she said.

"Why don't you try going with Freya then?" he suggested. "It can take some people a bit more time to figure it out."

Freya placed the sword gently at the base of the poem-wall, in front of the shield and the helmet. She chewed her lip. "I still can't believe they're coming to me. I hope I'm up to the task."

"You may be *the* One, Freya, but you're not the *only* one in this." Nyx placed a hand on her shoulder. "We're all here to help you."

"But first," Willow said brightly, "*you* need to help *me* warp. Come on."

Freya tucked her arm through Willow's. "Maybe it's easier for me because I'm not used to the vibrations?"

"Maybe. I know, let's try with me thinking of the pillar and you just keep your mind blank," Willow suggested.

They were within range of the vibrations now. "I dunno. It's kinda hard to *not* think of something, especially when you're trying not to," Freya said.

Willow's face was screwed up in concentration. All at once, they were travelling; then, just as suddenly, they landed with a thud beside the pillar.

"Willow, you did it," Freya enthused.

A woman screamed.

Freya spun. They weren't at the pillar near the Wastelands. They were in Konia.

Next to her, Willow panted heavily. She looked pleased with herself. "Yep, I sure did."

"You *meant* to bring us here?" Freya hissed.

Willow nodded and tugged Freya forwards. She waved at the woman who now stood clutching her shawl near her heart. "Hello, Mrs Baker," she said. Then over her shoulder to Freya she said, "I've got an idea."

Freya shook her head. "Your parents don't like me, remember?"

Last time they'd come here, Willow's parents had shunned Freya and forbidden Willow to help her. They'd even gone as far as to lock Willow in her room.

"I know. But Alex does."

Freya stopped dead in her tracks. Heat rose in her cheeks. "Alex? He's here?" she asked.

Willow winked at her. "I'm hoping so. Let's find out."

Chapter 6

ALEX

Willow marched out of the square, dragging Freya with her.

"Are you sure this is a good idea?" said Freya. "Brother Nyx asked—"

"Brother Nyx asked us to tell people about Adelpha," Willow interjected, "and that's exactly what we're going to do."

Freya's stomach did somersaults. "I'm not so sure—"

"Don't be such a mouse."

Freya's spirits lifted as Willow navigated them confidently to her house. Down one cobbled street, left at the next. Tidy brick houses lined the street like rows of teeth, set back from the road with gardens in front surrounded by low walls. Willow wasn't wrong, really. After all, Brother Nyx *had* asked them to tell people about Adelpha. Why not start with someone they knew?

When they arrived at Willow's house, Freya hung back. "Maybe I'll just wait out of sight."

Willow squeezed Freya's hand and tossed her head. "Actually, let's see if we can *both* avoid my parents." She pulled Freya around the side of the house to a window, reached up, and tapped a fingernail on it. Nothing happened. She tapped again. The curtain twitched aside and Alex peered out. Willow pressed her face and palms against the window. Alex yelped, and stumbled backwards.

Freya slapped a hand to her mouth, suppressing a laugh. He looked so funny.

Moments later, Alex joined them outside. "Willow, Freya. You're here. How are you? How *did* you get here? What happened after you got through that bat cave? Did you find the hermit?"

Willow raised her eyebrows. "That's a lot of questions, Alex. Good to see you, too." She smothered him in a bear hug.

"Yeah, you too, sis." He extracted himself from his twin's embrace and cut his eyes to Freya, a shy smile playing around his mouth. "Hi, Freya."

Freya's heart thumped. She smiled. "Hi Alex."

"Hey, the parents aren't home, are they?" Willow asked.

Alex shook his head. "No, won't be for another hour," he replied, glancing at the sun where it hung low in the sky.

"Well, in that case, let's go inside and we'll bring you up to speed over a nice cup of tea."

~

"So, here we are," Willow concluded, half an hour later, "warping around Tyrelia, getting ready to rescue Freya's family from the Golden City." She smiled smugly.

Freya rolled her eyes. "You make it sound like we're some sort of amazing heroes." She lifted a shoulder. "We're still just us, you know, and we've still got heaps to learn." She grinned wickedly. "Willow more than me, of course."

Willow punched her lightly on the arm, then turned to her brother. "So, what do you think?"

Alex blew his cheeks out. "It's cool. I don't care what you

say, it *is* amazing, what you're doing. I wish I could become an Adelphi, too."

"You can," Willow insisted. "Why do you think we came here?"

Alex pressed his mouth into a straight line. "Don't be ridiculous. What about Mother and Father?"

"What about them? Oh, I know. Looking after the sheep blah blah blah." Willow placed her palms flat on the table and leaned towards Alex. "This is bigger than sheep, Alex. This is life and death."

Alex blanched. "Well, if you put it like that …"

Willow sat back. "Tell you what. How about we just warp you to Adelpha, show you around, then bring you back here. Whaddaya say?"

Alex exhaled. He nodded once. "Sure. That would be great. Let's do it. I'll just leave a note in case you bring me back a bit late."

Willow leaped out of her chair and threw her arms around Alex. "You're gonna love this. Hope you don't get travel sick, though."

"What do you mean?"

"You'll see," Willow said.

A few moments later, they landed with a thump beside the Law Pillar in Adelpha. Alex stumbled to his knees, panting heavily. Freya patted him awkwardly on the shoulder.

"Are you all right?"

He nodded and got slowly to his feet. "Thanks for the warning." He gazed about him, taking in the forest then freezing as he spied the Temple. His eyes widened. "By the Ancient," he breathed. "It's real."

Willow nodded. "I couldn't believe it either, when I saw it." She pointed up to their left. "And see up there? That's the cave where we first met Brother Nyx—the hermit. The crack through to the bat cave is just along there a bit further."

Alex squinted at the cliff face. "Yes, I see. I think."

Freya ran towards the Temple. "We'd better introduce you to Brother Nyx."

Willow caught her twin's hand and led him inside. "You need to check out the poem." She dragged Alex to the far wall.

He sucked in his breath. "The Armour of Tyrelia. Can I touch it?"

"Sure," Willow said.

"Brother Nyx," Freya called, "We're back."

No response.

"Brother Nyx, where are you?" she called louder.

"I know. Let's call him on our talking stones," Willow suggested. "I'll do it. Watch this, Alex." She set her bright green talking stone flat on her palm. She squinted as she focussed her thoughts on it. A glowing green haze formed around the stone, shapes shifting and swirling until, within seconds, Nyx's face hung in the air. "Brother Nyx," Willow announced happily, "Freya and I are back. And we've brought someone with us."

Nyx's face registered surprise. "Is that so? Good, good. Where are you? I'll come and meet them."

"We're in the main atrium. See you soon."

Nyx's face disappeared, and Willow closed her fist around the stone.

Alex looked impressed. "That was really something."

"If you stay, you can learn how to do that, too." Willow said.

Shuffling footsteps and a tapping staff startled them. They whirled.

"Brother Nyx!" Willow's hand flew to her heart. "Already? That was quick. Let me introduce you to … Hang on a minute. Do you already know who this is?" she asked.

Nyx shuffled forward. "Why, yes, I do. Welcome, young Alex. Willow's twin, I believe?"

"How ...?"

Freya shook her head. "He did that with us, too. Brother Nyx, how *do* you do that?"

Nyx chuckled. "Why, your talking stone, of course."

Freya furrowed her brow. "I don't understand."

He gestured towards the pieces of Armour. "Remember where you got your stone from, Freya?"

"Yes, of course. It was in the centre of my shield—all those days when I couldn't contact the others, and the whole time I had a talking stone with me that I could've used." She shook her head, remembering her loneliness and despair, especially those first few days, before she'd met Willow.

Nyx lifted a finger. "Well, unbeknownst to you, you *were* using it."

"Huh?"

"You don't need to be holding the stone and looking at it for it to work. You were thinking about me, weren't you?"

"Of course. I was seeking 'the hermit'. That's *all* I was thinking about."

Nyx bobbed his head. "And so, your stone was activated. Mine began to glow and I could hear you talking to each other."

"Including hearing us using each other's names," said Willow.

Nyx smiled. "Now, Alex. Can I presume that Freya and Willow have explained what's at stake here now that you've agreed to become an Adelphi?"

Alex shot a look at Willow. "Not exactly."

"It's unusual, but not unheard of, for siblings to join the Order. But in such cases, it's very important that your parents are fully aware of the situation and have given their blessing for you both to commit to this path."

Willow was suddenly very interested in her feet.

Freya fidgeted with the hem of her tunic.

Nyx looked at Willow, then Freya, his eyebrows raised. "Would someone like to explain to me what's going on?"

"Our parents haven't exactly 'given their blessing' as you put it," Willow mumbled.

Nyx's chin shot up.

Alex shook his head. "No. More like we just informed them that we were coming here."

"And how did they take that?"

Willow dropped her head, blushing. "We didn't actually *talk* to them. Alex left them a note."

"Saying what?"

It was Alex's turn to blush. "Back soon," he said in a small voice.

Nyx tutted. "I suggest you warp him back now, Willow. And only return if your parents are agreeable."

Willow took a step back. "I can't," she protested.

"I'm sure your parents are more understanding than you give them credit for," Nyx replied.

Willow shook her head. "No, it's not that. I—I can't warp by myself yet. Freya warped us before."

"Is that so?" Nyx sighed. "This could all have been avoided if you were completely honest to start with."

"But she didn't lie," Freya said, defensively.

"Didn't she?" Nyx asked. "It sounds to me like she didn't tell the whole truth—either to her parents or to Alex. You didn't tell the whole truth either, Freya."

"Me?" Freya squeaked. "I didn't say anything. I've got even more reason to avoid Willow's parents than she does."

Nyx fixed her with his grey eyes. "No, you didn't say

anything," he agreed. "But you didn't stop her, either. So, you, too, were complicit in the subterfuge."

"Aren't you being a little dramatic?" Willow huffed. "What does it matter if we didn't tell the *whole* truth? It hasn't hurt anyone."

Nyx sighed. He lifted a finger to the poem on the wall, and quoted:

"Who is One who is honest and true?
Who has integrity in all they do?
Who does not play false, when they profess
Their 'no' is their 'no'; their 'yes' is their 'yes'.
Such a One, when lies are dealt
Shall receive the gift of the Belt

"It matters, because Freya is the One. Until she earns the Belt, she won't be ready to enter Medar. And if she doesn't enter Medar, then people *will* be hurt. Many, many people. Everyone in Medar, in fact, because they will never be able to come to Tyrelia."

Willow hung her head. "If you put it like that ..." she said in a small voice.

Nyx patted her hand. "I'll take you and Alex back to have a chat with your parents. See you soon, Freya."

~

Freya waited anxiously. What was taking so long? Would Alex come back? Would *Willow* come back? What if neither of them did? That would be awful. Everything had been going so well, until Brother Nyx had started going on about that honesty thing. He made it all sound so serious. Feeling shaky, she sank down at the base of the poem, next to her pieces of Armour. The light faded. She lay down, pillowing her head on her arms.

She dreamed she was wearing her Armour: her helmet and the shield. She was mounted on a white horse. She had an army. She turned to encourage them and brandished her sword above her head. "Attack!" she commanded, willing authority into her voice and facing her enemy once more: He was there, somewhere in the formidable Golden City. Suddenly, a solitary flaming arrow arced out of the topmost tier of the City, aiming straight for her. Wait! She hadn't earned the breastplate yet. And her shoes were missing. And the belt. The arrow continued its trajectory, on target to pierce her heart.

Well, she had proven false. Perhaps she deserved to die.

She jerked awake. Where was she? It was dark, and she was lying on a cold, hard floor. She heard voices. That's right. The Temple of the Adelphi. Brother Nyx was back. But who was with him? She leaped to her feet and followed the voices into the dining hall. They were all there: Brother Nyx, Willow and Alex.

She flung herself at Willow. "You came back." She gave Alex a quick hug. "You too. I was so worried you wouldn't." Her face grew hot. "I mean, I was worried neither of you would come back," she stammered, flustered.

Willow and Alex sported identical grins. "Yep, wouldn't miss it for anything," Willow said. "Turns out honesty really is the best policy. Come on. Let's eat."

"But first," Nyx interjected, "Alex needs to choose his stone. And I think I know just the one." He hobbled out of the room.

Alex, Willow and Freya exchanged glances before hurrying to follow him.

Chapter 7

RUBE'S REQUEST

Finally, Rube had spoken to Freya. *My daughter.* A warm glow flowed through his body. The revelation was still fresh. He had to get back into the Golden City straight away to tell Martha and Thomas that she was all right. *Her other parents.* They hadn't heard from Freya for weeks but, just last night, he'd spoken to her via the talking stones. She'd smashed hers within days of entering Tyrelia. *That* was why they hadn't heard from her. It had been such a relief to discover she was safe. More than safe, actually. She was training to become an Adelphi. Following in his footsteps. He smiled.

Even though he was invisible, he hated having to sneak in and out of the City. It was so risky, and his injured leg hampered his movements. Still, it had to be done. His talking stone didn't work inside the City, so he couldn't contact the others unless he was outside its walls.

He was almost at the drawbridge, when galloping hooves approached from behind. He leapt to the side, narrowly avoiding being flattened by a lone Guard on a horse. *What could that be about?*

He hurried over the bridge and through the gate, taking

advantage of the distraction to cover any noise he might make. Once through, he turned right then left, arriving soon after at the pretty whitewashed cottage where Freya's adoptive parents lived. The Games had finished, so Martha might be home. Or maybe she was next door at Hank and Leena's. He tiptoed to the rear of the house, then knocked quietly on the back door. No response. He pressed his ear against the wood and listened. He tried the knob. Locked. Next door then.

Soon he was inside Hank and Leena's house.

"She's not here, Rube," Leena said. "Hank took her to the printing press."

"Wasn't that a bit dangerous?" Rube asked, recalling his opportune springing of Thomas from prison just last night, and their timely decision to hide him—all without knowing that Jack was scheming behind their backs.

Leena waved a hand. "She couldn't wait to see Thomas," she explained.

Rube knew where the printing press was. Hank had a secret room in his office, the entrance hidden behind a filing cabinet. It was there that he had secured the book about Tyrelia, which Rube had stolen from the Master's mansion. Then, when Rube had rescued Thomas from prison, they'd hidden him there too. "I've got to tell her the good news: we've contacted Freya—"

Leena threw her arms around him. "Oh my, that's such a relief," she said.

"—and she's found the leader of the Adelphi in Tyrelia. I'll tell you all about it when I get back," Rube finished, patting Leena's arm.

He crept down to Hank's printing press. Checking that nobody was around, he slipped inside the dim interior. Being Saturday, the place was deserted. He limped between the shadowy shapes of two massive printing machines. A faint line of light framed the door at the rear of the room. Rube tapped lightly on the wood. "Hank," he called.

"Who's there?" a gruff voice asked.

"It's me, Rube." The door opened and Rube entered, visible now. "I take it Martha's down there with Thomas?" he asked, inclining his head towards an unassuming four-drawer filing cabinet behind Hank.

Hank's grin was barely visible amongst the bushy hair that covered his face. "She sure is. Do you want to join them?" He pulled a face that said *you really don't want to go down there.*

Rube laughed. "Maybe I'll wait a bit, then," he said.

Suddenly, they heard a door slam from the main printing press.

"Someone's here," Hank hissed.

Rube instantly turned himself invisible. Not a moment too soon.

The office door flung open and a Guard burst into the room. His eyes fastened on Hank. "Are you alone here?" he barked.

Rube took a careful step backwards.

Hank nodded. "Uh, yes sir, I am," he said. He looked like a kid caught with his hand in the cookie jar, Rube thought.

"Where's Martha Farmer?" the Guard demanded.

Hank shrugged his shoulders. "I'm not sure," he said. "At her home, maybe?"

"She was seen coming in here with you." The Guard poked Hank in the chest.

"Oh." Hank was at a loss.

The Guard strode towards Hank and gripped his arm. "You're coming with me for questioning," he said. He yanked Hank towards the door.

Hank stumbled after him, stammering "Where are you taking me?" The door slammed shut.

Remaining invisible, Rube tiptoed to the filing cabinet and slipped his fingers between it and the wall, sliding them carefully down about halfway. Something clicked and the whole cabinet swung outwards, revealing a door.

"Martha, Thomas," he called hoarsely. "It's me, Rube."

Martha and Thomas appeared at the bottom of a flight of stairs, illuminated by a candle. "What was all that yelling about?" Martha called.

"Hank's just been taken away by a Guard," Rube shot back. "I have so much to tell you, but I really need to go and find out where they're taking him. I think it's best if you stay here. I'll leave this door unlatched." He waved a hand in the direction of the filing cabinet.

Martha nodded, wringing her hands. "Okay, Rube. Stay safe."

Rube hurried out of the room, through the main warehouse, and slipped out on to the street. Nobody around. Good. Now, where was that Guard? Chances were, they were taking Hank down to the Guard's quarters near the Level One gate. It was roughly the same direction as Hank's house, so maybe he'd detour to check there on the way. He set off at a fast hobble, careful to stick to the shadows.

Before long, he arrived at Hank and Leena's house. It was dark and quiet. Nobody home. He continued to the Guard's quarters. Ah, there was Hank up ahead, still being marched hard by the Guard. He picked up his pace.

He was too late to slip inside behind Hank, so he loitered outside under a window, hoping to hear something. No such luck. Just as he was about to leave, the door opened again, and out came Hank, Leena and young Sam, their son, escorted by four Guards. By the Land, what was going on? Leena gripped Sam's hand tightly.

"Are we really going to shift to Level Two?" Sam asked, his eight-year-old voice high with excitement.

Leena dropped a kiss on her son's curly head. "It seems so, Sam. Apparently they need your da to manage the printing press there. Although I don't know why it couldn't wait until morning." She glared at the Guard to her left.

Rube trailed behind them as far as their turn off, then hurried back to the printing press. It was dusk now, and the shadowy streets became his friend. He slipped back inside the building and ran to the hidden chamber. Careful not to let the cabinet click shut behind him, he descended into the small room where Thomas had been hiding the past four days.

"First of all, Freya is alive and well," he announced to Thomas and Martha.

Martha clasped her hands together. "You've spoken to her?" she asked, her eyes shining.

"Yes. It turned out she'd smashed her talking stone. That's why we couldn't contact her. She's had quite an adventure in Tyrelia and, with the help of a friend, Willow, she found Brother Nyx, the head of my Order. She's training to become an Adelphi, too."

"Is she going to bring us the Helix River water, then?" asked Thomas.

Using the book he'd stolen from the Master's library, Rube had deduced that water from the headwaters of the Helix River was an antidote to the injections that kept the inhabitants of the Golden City trapped. He'd shared this discovery with Martha, Hank, Leena, Jack and Sam right before Jack had tried to betray him. Later, Brother Nyx had confirmed that the water was indeed the key to allowing the inhabitants of the Golden City to leave.

He scratched his chin. "Not exactly. Brother Nyx insists that she needs to learn various skills, including mastering the art of invisibility, before she can come back to Medar. So, it might be some time before you're rescued. Sorry."

"How long?" Martha asked. "I mean, we're doing alright with Thomas being hidden here, but … Jack bought his way up to Level Two today. He's gone already."

Rube sighed. "Hank, Leena and Sam are being forced to move up to Level Two right now. Things are going to get tricky."

"What?" Martha pressed her hands together. "Can Thomas stay here, do you think?"

"I really don't know," Rube replied. "For now, I think it's best if I take you back home. Then I need to get outside the City before the gates close to talk to the other Watchers. See if we can speed things up."

Rube waited in Hank's office while Martha said goodnight to Thomas. Then, turning himself and Martha invisible, he escorted her back home. He sneaked out of the City as the last light faded.

Crossing the drawbridge, the *tramp, tramp, tramp* of marching feet filled the air. A column of Guards was exiting the City behind him. He scurried off the drawbridge and leapt to the side just in time. What could that be about? Rubbing his hip, he hurried to his usual copse of bushes and fished out his talking stone. First, he called Saff.

"I was just trying to call you," Saff said from the red swirl in Rube's palm.

Rube narrowed his eyes. "Why's that?"

"The bridge rebuild was going very well. Until today. We were attacked by Guards and one got away," Saff said.

That explained the bedraggled Guard he'd seen fleeing into the City that morning, and the troupe of Guards exiting the

City.

"More Guards are on their way, Saff. I saw them leaving the City just now. A long column of them," Rube said urgently.

"Thanks for the warning, my friend. We'll see what we can do to prepare for the attack."

Rube closed his hand around the stone, cutting off the communication. He frowned. Then he opened his palm and concentrated his thoughts once more. Shortly, Freya's face swirled in the red haze.

"Hello ... Father," she said. "You'll never guess what happened today."

Rube smiled, despite himself. "What happened, Freya?"

"I learned to warp. And I earned the Sword!"

"By the Master, that's incredible," he said. "But ... what is 'warping'?"

"It's travelling between Law Pillars," Freya said, surprised. "Except Brother Nyx doesn't need the pillars. Today, I did four trips with Brother Nyx, one by myself and one with Willow." She bit her lip, as if to stop herself saying more.

"So, would you be able to 'warp' here, to the Golden City?"

Freya shook her head. "I don't think I can—unless there's a pillar there. I don't know about Brother Nyx. Besides, your stone doesn't work in the City. Maybe warping doesn't either."

Rube closed his eyes. He thought a moment. "Did you say that these pillars are everywhere in Tyrelia? Where's the closest one, do you think?"

"I'd have to check with Brother Nyx but, from what I saw on the map, I guess the one near the Alpha gate—you know, where the Cave People and the broken bridge are."

Rube scratched his chin. *That might work.* "Do you think Brother Nyx could warp there and get some Helix Water to Saff and Thyst?"

"I don't know. Why the urgency?"

"Saff and Thyst have begun to rebuild the Alpha bridge, but the Master has discovered what they're up to. Guards are on their way right now. They'll arrive there late tomorrow. If we can't get the water to Saff by tomorrow morning, we might not get another chance."

Freya's mouth dropped open.

"But that's not all," Rube added.

"Has something happened to my family?" Freya asked.

Rube jerked his head. "Things are getting … complicated here. Everyone's fine," he reassured her, "but Jack has bought his way up to Level Two and now your parents' neighbours have been forced to move up, too. I'm worried about your mother, Freya. I'm not sure how she'll cope with these latest developments. And of course, now that Hank's gone, we'll probably have to shift Thomas. I really don't know how we're going to continue to keep him safe. We need to get them out of the Golden City. Fast."

"You'd better talk to Brother Nyx. I'll go find him so I can listen." She disappeared.

Within seconds, Nyx's face swirled above Rube's palm.

"No," Nyx said flatly, once Rube had explained everything. "They aren't ready. I must stay here and train them. What if I leave and something happens to me? We can't risk the fate of all people in Medar for just a few in the Golden City. We need more time."

"But—" Rube started.

"No," Nyx repeated. "My acolytes haven't mastered invisibility. It's imperative that they do. And we need to recruit more. You'll just have to wait."

Rube stared blankly at his talking stone. Brother Nyx had gone. What was he going to do?

Chapter 8

HELIX WATER

Freya paced back and forth in their small bedroom.

"Will you stop doing that, please?" Willow begged from where she sat on her bed next to her brother. "You're making me dizzy."

"I have to *do* something, Willow," Freya fretted. "I have to help my family get out of that city."

"You heard the old man: *My young acolytes are not ready. I can't leave them,*" Willow mimicked.

Freya sighed and dropped onto her bed, burying her head in her hands.

Alex raised an eyebrow at Willow. Pushing himself away from the wall, he placed a hand on Freya's shoulder. "Hey, don't give up. Maybe we're looking at this all wrong."

Freya lifted her head, her long fringe tickling her cheek. "What do you mean?"

"Well," Alex said, leaning against the wall again. "Sure, Brother Nyx still has a lot to teach us, so we probably shouldn't go. And sure, Willow and I haven't mastered warping properly. But you have."

Freya crossed her arms. "But Brother Nyx said we shouldn't

go. And I can't make myself invisible yet."

Willow jabbed a finger at Freya. "*You* may not have mastered invisibility. But didn't you say that those other Watchers have? Saff and Thyst?"

"So, you're suggesting I get the water to *them*, and they get it into the City?"

Willow and Alex both nodded.

"I don't know …"

"You wouldn't be going anywhere *near* the Golden City. You'd just be making sure the water got there," Willow pointed out.

"I suppose," Freya conceded. "We'd need to make sure Brother Nyx doesn't find out, though."

Alex glanced at his twin. "Leave that with us. We're pretty practised at distraction." He winked.

"I bet you are," Freya said, smiling.

"Tell you what," Willow said, "I'll go up to the cave and get the water. After all, I'm faster than you and I know exactly where to go."

Freya remembered the hermit giving her a cup of water to drink in the cave as part of her ceremony to become a citizen of Tyrelia. It seemed so long ago now. "Thanks, Willow," she said. "Are you sure, though? It's getting pretty dark."

"All the more reason. I have two good eyes, and I can always use my talking stone to light the way. Although, being able to warp to that cave would be pretty handy right now." Her voice was muffled as she pulled a jumper over her head. "Right, see you both soon."

With Willow gone, the room felt small. Like she was too close to Alex.

He wriggled. "Umm, I think I'll go with Willow," he blurted. "I've never seen the cave. Might be a good opportunity."

"Yeah, sure," Freya said. "Good idea."

Alex leaped up and left the room.

Freya puffed out her cheeks. Her heart was beating really fast. Weird. She flopped down on her bed to wait.

~

Alex ran into the main atrium. Willow wasn't there. He went outside and stood on the steps, scanning the clearing. The moon was rising from behind the mountain. He spotted a dark shape entering the trees. "Willow," he whispered, not wanting Brother Nyx or Hilda to hear him. Unfortunately, Willow can't have heard him either, as she kept going.

Alex ran lightly down the stairs, across the grass, and into the darkness of the forest. "Willow," he called again.

She spun, her hand against her chest. "Alex! You gave me a fright. What are you doing here?"

"I thought I'd keep you company. I haven't seen this cave and thought it might be cool to check it out."

Willow nodded curtly. "Alright, let's go then."

It took them a good hour to climb the zig-zag path to the cave. They were both sweating by the time they got there. Alex turned. The moon bathed the valley in a silver light. Thousands of leaves, in varying shades of grey, hid the Temple from view. Black silhouettes of the mountains ringed the secret valley, like a giant bat concealing them within the circle of its wings. He let out a low whistle. "What a view."

Willow grunted. "I suppose."

Turning to follow her into the cave, a mural on the wall caught Alex's eye. He took a step closer to inspect it. He called to Willow, who'd moved deeper into the cave. "Did you see this painting?"

"Sure," Willow said, turning back to him. "Oh. It's

changed."

Alex glanced at her. "How?"

"Well, when we first arrived here, I could've sworn it was the outline of just one person. But now there are three figures. And what are they holding?"

"Maybe Brother Nyx has been coming up here to paint."

Willow pulled a face. "He must've, I guess. But he's been pretty busy with us the whole time. I'm not sure when he would've managed it."

Alex shrugged. "Maybe it's another mystical skill we have yet to learn."

"Maybe," she said. Suddenly, a faint green glowed from the stone in the palm of her hand. "That's better." She continued deeper into the cave, skirting some chairs and a low table to pass through into an adjoining chamber.

Alex pulled out his own stone: alexandrite. He focused on it and, within seconds, a pale-yellow halo formed around it. He followed his sister cautiously. Soon he heard running water.

"Throw some light over here, please," Willow said over her shoulder. She shoved her stone into a pocket and pulled a waterskin out of another.

Alex held his stone as close to the water as he dared. Willow carefully positioned the mouth of the skin into the small waterfall flowing down the rockface. The skin swelled as it filled. Willow pushed a cork into the top then flicked the skin. Drops of icy water sprayed his face.

"Stop it. That's cold," he said.

Willow slung the skin over her shoulder and rubbed her hands on her trousers. "*You're* cold," she scoffed. "Try holding your hands in it like I did." Taking out her talking stone, she said, "I'll just let Freya know that we've got it and are on our way back."

~

As the first rays of dawn tinged the mountain peak, Freya crept out of the Temple. The vibrations of the Law Pillar called her. She placed a hand on the rough timber of the temple door. With any luck, she would be back before Brother Nyx even discovered she'd gone. She tiptoed into the shimmering air and was sucked into a vortex. *The Alpha gate, the Alpha gate.* Suddenly, the vibrations ceased, and she stumbled onto a grassy plain. Was she in the right place? Nothing was familiar. Ah, an archway. That was promising.

She waded towards it, the dew from the tall grass soaking her leggings. Her heart beat faster. If this was the correct gate, Saff and Thyst were not far away. It would be good to see them again. She broke into a run, the waterskin thumping on her hip.

Near the archway, she slowed to a walk. The sun's early morning rays glinted off the almost-transparent, roughly hewn rocks. She clenched her fists, remembering passing through the Beta gate, all those weeks ago. She stepped through the archway and stopped, almost expecting another shield to magically appear on her back. She tossed her head. Of course, passing through the Beta gate had been an act of obedience. What she was doing now was one of disobedience. Maybe, back at the Temple, the shield had disappeared? She shuddered. Hesitated. No, nothing she could do about it now. There were more important tasks at hand. Like helping to rescue her family from the Golden City.

She covered the short distance to the edge of the Chasm and scanned the lip. There—the stairs. It was too dim to see if anyone was below. She began her descent.

The stairs were ancient and crumbling. Nobody had used them in a thousand years, so it was to be expected. She'd better call Saff, as arranged late last night. She sat down on a step and pulled out her talking stone from the pouch hanging around her neck. She focussed her thoughts on him, and before long the multi-coloured hue took on his features. "I'm here, Saff," she said happily. "I'm just climbing down the staircase."

"Excellent," he responded. "Thyst and I will go down now. See you soon."

By the time she reached the bottom, her legs were shaking, and she sat down for a moment to recover. She massaged her thighs. At least her leggings were a bit drier now. A warmth seeped into her chest, just below her throat. Someone was calling her. It was Thyst.

"Good morning, Freya. We're here. We can see you."

Freya whipped her head up and squinted across the Chasm. Directly opposite, a faint purple light shone. "I can see your stone-glow."

"Make your way to the bridge. We've only managed to build two sections to span the gap, but Saff's going to come across to you. Just wait at the end of the logs, okay?"

Freya nodded her understanding. Holding her stone in front of her to light the way, she stepped onto the stone bridge deck. It was wide with rails either side. Perfectly safe. Shortly, she reached the logs. She strained to see Saff. She consulted her stone. "I can't see Saff, where is he?"

"He's just crawled onto the logs. You should see him soon."

Freya extinguished her stone. She blinked. Her eye adjusted to the gloom. There! That must be him. Suddenly, a yell from one of the Cavemen echoed through the Chasm. Freya immediately reconnected with Thyst. "What was that?" she asked.

"I'm not sure. Let me find out." Thyst cut off the communication.

Freya's dug her fingernails into her palms. Saff was

crawling so slowly. What was going on with that yell? She willed her stone to grow warm. Another minute ticked by. At last, she felt the familiar warmth from the stone clenched in her fist. She opened her palm to reveal Thyst's face swirling in her stone-glow. "What is it?" Freya asked.

Thyst shook her head, her eyes worried. "It's the Guards. They must've marched all night. They've nearly reached the edge of the forest. I'm sorry, Freya, I think you're going to have to go out to meet Saff."

Freya gulped. She nodded solemnly. "Alright, Thyst. I'll do it." She tucked her stone back into its pouch and crouched, placing her palms on the logs. They felt solid enough. She wiped her hands briefly on her tunic, then lifted first one knee, then the other, onto the logs. She had only crawled a short distance when the logs sagged slightly under her weight. She froze, her knuckles white as she gripped one of the twine ropes.

Thyst shouted. Freya glanced up in time to see Thyst turn herself invisible.

"Freya," Saff called, an undertone of urgency in his voice.

She squeezed her eyes shut. "I can't go any further, Saff. These logs are too flimsy." She imagined the plunging drop beneath her. A cold sweat pricked her brow.

"Can you throw the waterskin to me?" Saff stood up, steadying himself with his arms.

Freya lifted her head. He was ten metres away. Or maybe only five? It was hard to tell in this gloom and with only one eye.

"I don't know," Freya said, her voice trembling.

"You can do it. You don't have to stand up, just stay on your knees," he suggested.

She sat on her heels. Wasn't he still too far away? "Are you sure?" she asked.

He stepped towards her. "Yes, Freya. Throw it now!"

She unslung the waterskin and wrapped the cord around it. "Ready?" she called. Holding it in her palm, she reached back behind her right ear. Then she flung her arm forward. The waterskin left her hand and sailed through the air in a high arc. No! It was too far to the right.

Saff took another step forward, his eyes fastened on the prize. His foot rolled off the log and he landed heavily on his left knee. Lunging, he snagged the cord as the waterskin bounced off the trunks in front of him. He fell flat on his stomach, his arm extended into the Chasm, the waterskin dangling from his fingers.

"Got it," he said. But then he grunted. "Freya, help!"

Freya's relief shredded into tatters.

Saff scrabbled to hold on to the trees, but instead ripped off a piece of bark. His anguished cry rang in her ears, echoing in the Chasm as he plummeted to the depths, clutching the bark and the waterskin.

"No," Freya screamed. "Saff." She flung herself forward, her arm outstretched into the Chasm, her hand splayed. But it was hopeless. She was too far away. "Saff," she screamed once more. His diminishing form, surrounded by his fluttering cloak, with his arm reaching for her, was swallowed by the gloomy depths. She rolled back onto the logs, sobbing. What had she done? In a daze, she scrabbled backwards to the safety of the platform. She didn't stop until she had climbed the stairs and reached the archway. She crawled up to it and leaned against it as the morning rays lightened the sky. Tears streamed down her face. *Saff.* Great, heaving sobs wracked her frame. Gradually, they slowed to hiccoughs. She rubbed her eyes. Her breathing returned to normal. She had to tell someone.

"Willow," she cried the minute she connected with her

friend.

"What is it, Freya? What's wrong?" Willow's eyes were full of concern.

"I—I— Saff's gone," she finally blurted. "Guards came, and I had to throw the waterskin and he caught it but … it was a bad throw, and he fell off the bridge into the Chasm." Tears overwhelmed her once more.

"Where are you now?" Willow asked. "Are you okay?"

Freya nodded and wiped her eyes. "Yes. I'm at the Alpha Gate. I guess … I guess I should come home."

"You do that, Freya. Come back now."

Freya tucked her stone away. She got up. The walk across the meadow seemed twice as far as when she'd arrived. Numbly, she allowed herself to be consumed by the humming vibrations. She stumbled out of the vortex at the pillar at Adelpha, straight into Willow's arms.

Willow held her tightly as she sobbed.

"Hush now, Freya," Willow soothed. "It'll be all right."

"No," Freya wailed, the word muffled against Willow's shoulder. She spun away, her fists clenched at her sides. "How can it be all right? Saff's dead, and I lost the water. We'll *never* rescue my family now. Why did I ever think I could do it? Brother Nyx was right. I'm not ready. I've let *everyone* down. I'm not worthy of their sacrifices."

Brother Nyx hobbled up to her. He laid his hand on her arm. "My child," he said in his wheezy voice. "I'm so sorry. But all is not lost."

Freya sniffed. "What do you mean, 'all is not lost'? *Everything's* lost. Because of me." She wailed once more.

Nyx's eyes were fierce under his bushy brows. "Oh, my child." He sighed. "You are so young and have so much yet to learn. Yes, we lost a brother today. But he is not the first, and certainly won't be the last. You mustn't blame yourself. Yes, you lost a pouch of Helix water. But there is plenty more where that came from." He waved his arm overhead, in the general direction of the cave. "Many people made decisions that culminated in this tragedy. Not just you." He wagged a finger at her. "And we can make new choices that can rectify the situation."

Freya cocked her head. She sniffed again. "What new choices?" she asked in a small voice.

He tapped a finger against his nose. "Come inside where it's not so chilly and I'll tell you." He hobbled off towards the Temple. Freya trailed him, supported by Willow.

Chapter 9

THYST

Thyst dashed up the stairs, two at a time. She paused at the top, gauging her entry into the battle at the surface. It was chaos. The clearing between the Chasm and the trees heaved with Guards and Cavemen, the former slashing with swords, the latter ducking and darting, stabbing their daggers at their foe's legs. A row of Cavemen archers, positioned off to one side, shot their poisoned arrows into the fray, but many bounced off the Guards' armour without inflicting damage.

She ducked as a Guard and Caveman, locked together, pounded past her. Then, still invisible, she slipped over the lip, skirting the fighting, and joined the archers. She nocked an arrow but couldn't lock onto a target: she was just as likely to take down a Caveman as a Guard. Her dagger, then. Not her preferred weapon, but she knew how to use it. She ran to the forest fringe. A Guard, frantically fighting a Caveman, backed towards her. She neatly thrust her dagger between the Guard's ribs and he dropped at her feet. The Caveman's eyes widened at the unexpected demise of his foe, but he instantly turned to rejoin the fight.

Sticking to the treeline, she dispatched two more unwary

Guards. She stabbed her blade into the ground to clean off the blood, but she needn't have bothered. At that moment, a Guard stumbled over a tree root, landing next to where she crouched. She slit his throat with a single fluid motion. Hot droplets splattered her face. She stared at his dull grey skin. Ugh, rotten. She spat, more to clear her revulsion than the blood.

A shout caught her attention. What had happened? She leapt to her feet and ran to the edge of the Chasm. A group of Cavemen were racing down the stairs, gesturing at the bridge below. *Oh no.* Five or six Guards were clustered around the end of the logs, hacking at the ropes. How had they got there? She followed the Cavemen. One flight, two flights, three flights. It was taking too long. Finally, they burst out onto the bridge platform, the Cavemen howling. Three of the Guards spun to confront them, swords raised. The Cavemen ducked and darted, attempting to use their diminutive stature to their advantage, but the bridge rails either side hampered their movements, and they couldn't get past. Thyst ran back to the stairs and stood on the second to bottom one. She unslung her bow, nocked an arrow and took aim. There. The left-most Guard crumpled to the ground, Thyst's arrow protruding from his forehead.

With a shout, the Cavemen surged forwards, leaping over the dead Guard, but it was too late. At the same time, with a grunt and a mighty shove, the three remaining Guards pushed the logs into the Chasm. *No! Not the new bridge.* With renewed fury, the Cavemen attacked the Guards. One of the Cavemen charged a Guard, and they both toppled into the Chasm, screaming as they fell. The remaining Cavemen each lined up a target and did likewise. Within moments, none were left. Thyst allowed herself to become visible and slumped onto the step. Gone. They were all gone. Saff and Freya—where were they? She leapt to her feet and ran to the edge of the platform, peering across to the other side. Her eyes traced the stairs all the way to the top of the opposite cliff, but there was no sign of movement. Maybe Saff was here somewhere, invisible. She dashed back up the stairs.

~

Thyst fumbled her talking stone from the pouch at her belt. Finally, someone was calling her. It had been hours since the bridge incident. She hoped it was Saff. But the swirling purple haze resolved into the features of another man. "Brother Nyx." She dipped her head in acknowledgement of his status. "It's good to hear from you. From someone. Do you know where Saff and Freya are?"

Nyx forced a tight smile. "Freya's safe. She's here with me now. Saff … I'm sorry, my child. He is with us no more."

Thyst's vision blurred and she suddenly couldn't breathe. *Saff!* "Wha—what do you mean?"

"He tumbled off the bridge trying to secure the waterskin," he said.

Thyst squeezed her eyes shut and leant her head back against the cave wall. Tears leaked from under her lashes, tracing wet trails down her cheeks. She took several deep breaths and rubbed her sleeve across her face. After a moment, she addressed Nyx once more. "So," she said shakily, "all hope is lost."

"No, my child, it is not," he replied firmly. "I should reprimand you all for going against my wishes … but there is no point. No. Even had today's tragedy not occurred, the Master is making his move, and I see now that we must make haste. There is another way."

A kernel of hope sparked in her chest. "There is?"

Nyx nodded. "Tell me, child, where are you now?"

"I'm here hiding in the caves with the Cave People. What's left of them, anyhow."

"Tell me, please?"

"It all happened so fast. The Guards arrived much sooner than expected. All the fighting men raced up top, but it was a slaughter. The only reason they didn't get me is because I was invisible." Thyst gulped a breath of air. "Somehow, a group of Guards managed to get to the bridge. They've destroyed all our work. They hacked all the ropes and pushed the logs into the Chasm. So, I returned to the caves to see if I could find Saff and protect the others. I gathered a group in a sleeping cave—one that's only accessible by a ladder from the cave below. I pulled up the ladder, made everyone hold their neighbour's hand, and turned us all invisible. At one stage, a Guard stuck his head up the hole, but luckily the baby didn't cry, and he declared the room empty. Eventually, when there were no more sounds of disturbance, I ventured out. I couldn't find Saff. I was hoping … I thought maybe Saff had made it across and was in Tyrelia with Freya."

Nyx shook his head sadly. "I'm afraid not. Freya wants to know why you thought Saff might be in Tyrelia? She tells me that he couldn't pass through the Wall."

"Oh," Thyst explained. "He believes. I mean, believed," she corrected. She blinked rapidly. "He saw Tyrelia—right after the Guards came that first time. He believed," she repeated.

"Then he truly is not lost," Nyx said.

"I don't understand."

"He died knowing the truth. Not believing in a lie. Even though he never made it to Tyrelia in person, he was there in his heart."

Thyst sniffed and nodded. It was a comforting thought.

"Now, do you know where the obelisk is in the Shady

Desert?"

"What?" she asked. She ran a hand through her hair. "Roughly, but I've never been there. Why?"

"You can't stay where you are. Freya and I will meet you at the obelisk with a new skin of water."

Thyst nearly dropped her stone. "How?" she asked.

"Oh," Nyx said, matter-of-fact, "the obelisk is a Law Pillar. We can warp there."

Thyst exhaled. Her thoughts whirled. If there was a Law Pillar there, were there more in Medar? Would Brother Nyx be able to warp them all closer to the Golden City? It would be difficult, having to constantly maintain contact with Freya if she wasn't able to make herself invisible. It had been hard enough with three able-bodied Watchers to maintain Freya's invisibility, let alone with only one. By all accounts, Rube was still injured, and Brother Nyx hobbled about with the aid of a staff. "But I thought you said Freya's not ready?" she blurted.

"She's not," Nyx confirmed, "and she certainly won't be going anywhere by herself until she masters invisibility."

"What exactly are you suggesting?"

"I'll warp Freya to the obelisk to ensure we're not seen. We give the skin to you. You take it to the Golden City."

"Oh, right. Me." Thyst's heart thudded. *Me? I can't. But I have to. There's only two Watchers left in Medar to help Freya. Saff wouldn't hesitate.* "Any idea how long it should take me to get to this pillar?"

Nyx bobbed his head. "Have you got your horse?"

"Yes."

"I've consulted my maps. I estimate the journey should take you around four days. The obelisk is due north when you're half-way between Yawside and Yawbridge."

"Okay." Another thought occurred to her. "What about

Rube? Have you managed to contact him yet? Does he know about …" she swallowed hard and blinked rapidly.

Nyx's eyes filled with compassion. "Not yet," he said. "I can call him now and tell him about Saff, if you like?"

Thyst quickly shook her head. She brushed her eyes with the heel of her free hand. "I need to talk to him anyhow. I'll do it. Shall we stick to our previous arrangement and contact each other daily at sunset?"

"Yes, my dear. Safe travels and talk tonight. Oh, one more thing. Freya says that, when you get there, do NOT go inside the obelisk."

Thyst smiled wryly. "I remember." *I remember Saff telling me about the gnomes infesting the tunnels deep underground. Oh, Saff. My love.* "Goodbye, Brother Nyx." She closed her fingers over her stone, extinguishing the purple glow.

Chapter 10

NEW RECRUITS

Freya, Willow, Alex, and Brother Nyx gathered beside the Law Pillar.

"This time when I warp you to Heneva, I'd like you to tell people about Medar. About how we need more acolytes to join the Order, so they can help rescue their people," Nyx instructed.

Freya shook her head. "I don't think I can do it, Brother Nyx."

He peered at her. "Of course you can."

"But—but what if I mess up again? I caused Saff's death. What if someone else gets hurt?" She turned away.

Nyx laid a hand on her arm. "Freya," he said gently, "failing in a task doesn't mean you should give up, and it certainly doesn't make you a failure. Not everything works out the first time. Sometimes you just need to keep trying different approaches."

She hung her head.

"Remember what I told you about being able to offset poor choices in the past with better choices in the future?"

She lifted her chin and nodded.

"This is one of those choices, Freya."

Deep inside her, something clicked. She had a choice. She could start to make things better. She wasn't a failure—unless she gave up. Well, she wasn't going to do that. Not on her family, and not on Thyst. "What do we need to do?"

"We go to Heneva. Hands on my shoulders, like we practised."

They stepped into the vibrations and, before Freya could blink, they landed at the Law Pillar in the middle of Heneva.

It was busy. Being mid-morning, the market was in full swing. Rows of stalls filled the central plaza, the tables stacked with a multitude of goods: fresh and cooked food, livestock and poultry in one aisle; clothing, jewellery and shoes in the middle; and handcrafted homewares such as pottery, basketware, silverware and haberdashery on the other. All sorts of nick-nacks and artworks were scattered in between. Somewhere at the back, minstrels played a lively tune. It was a sea of colour, sounds, smells, and activity.

Several people enjoyed a quiet moment relaxing on the steps of the plinth of the Law Pillar, sipping drinks, eating food, and soaking up the atmosphere.

Without warning, Nyx allowed Freya's group to become visible.

A small child standing nearby squealed in fright, burst into tears, and clutched at his mother's leg, burying his face in her skirts. "Hush," she soothed, turning to see what had scared her child so. She yelped, stepping backwards. "Where did you come from?"

Brother Nyx leaned on his staff, and raised a hand to signal … what? Peace? Quiet? Freya wasn't sure, but the people calmed down.

"Brothers and sisters," he called, "I am Brother Nyx, the

leader of the Adelphi, and I am here to announce to you today that the Order is alive and well."

Several people gasped, and a low murmur ran through the onlookers. The crowd grew as more people came to find out what was happening.

"Adelphi?" Freya heard someone say. "Thought they'd all died."

"What's a delphy?" another asked.

"The Adelphi are here first and foremost to serve the Ancient. We have learned how to discern his voice and tap into his powers," Nyx declared.

"What sort of powers?" a woman called.

Nyx bobbed his head. "We can warp between Law Pillars and turn ourselves invisible," he stated.

"You can not," a man scoffed, turning away. "What a waste of time," he muttered. He shouldered his way through the crowd.

Nyx spun. He placed his hand on Freya's arm. She guessed his intention and quickly grabbed Willow's hand. Willow was still linked with Alex. They instantly disappeared.

The crowd gasped collectively, and the man turned back.

Nyx allowed them to become visible once more.

A few people clapped and cheered.

Nyx scowled and hobbled forward. "This is no circus trick," he roared, thumping his staff on the marble plinth.

The clapping petered out.

Nyx glowered at the throng. He shook his head wearily. "My children, *that* was the power of the Ancient. I know many of you have forgotten what the Ancient has done for us. We take it for granted that we have an abundance of food. That our Laws and Rules are good. That we live in peace and harmony, not oppressed. But this is not the case for all people."

"Who's oppressed, then?" a woman demanded.

Nyx beckoned Freya forward. "The people in Medar," he announced. "The Hole."

The noise swelled.

Nyx motioned for quiet. "This is Freya," he said, "and she is from Medar."

"She doesn't look any different from us," the woman retorted. "How do we know she's from *there*?"

"No, she doesn't look different now," Brother Nyx agreed. "But before she took the vow to become a citizen of Tyrelia and drank the Helix water, she looked quite different. Her skin was not translucent. She is changed."

"It's true," Willow stepped forward to stand beside Freya. "I was there. I saw it."

"And who are you?" a man asked.

Nyx waggled a hand in their direction. "These are my acolytes. They have taken up the challenge to train to become Adelphi. They are willing to follow the Ancient's call to enter Medar and tell the people there about Tyrelia." Nyx swept his gaze across the crowd. "Who here is willing to follow the call? Who here has the courage to go to Medar?"

A low mutter filled the quiet. People shuffled their feet and glanced uncertainly at their neighbours. Some at the back drifted off. Others suddenly realised they had urgent shopping to do and departed, making excuses. Before long the crowd had dispersed. Except for one lad.

"Hello, young man. What's your name?" Nyx asked.

"Peregrine, sir," he said. "Is it true, about the Hole? That people live in there?"

Nyx nodded solemnly. "Yes, it is."

The lad pressed his mouth into a tight line. He was tall and lanky with straight brown hair. "Alright, then. I'd like to become one of them." He inclined his head towards Freya, Willow and Alex. "What did you call them?"

Nyx smiled. "An acolyte of the Order of the Adelphi. How old are you, Peregrine?"

"Eighteen, sir."

"Good." Nyx grunted. "Go tell your parents of your decision. We'll return tomorrow, same time."

"Don't have any parents, sir," he said. "But I'll let my grandmother know. See you tomorrow." He ran off.

~

When they warped back to Heneva to get Peregrine, he had brought his friend Tarek.

"Can you tell Tarek what you told me, sir?" Peregrine asked.

Nyx turned to his acolytes. "Which of you would like to have a go?"

Alex nudged Willow. Willow poked her tongue out at him, and shoved Freya forward.

"Ah, Freya. Very good." Nyx nodded approvingly.

Freya shot an indignant look at Willow before facing the young men. "I … uh … my name's Freya and I'm from Medar. The Hole." *Where to start?* She lifted her head and inhaled deeply. "Before I came to Tyrelia, I had never smelled the sea. We don't have oceans in Medar. We're surrounded by a Chasm and Wall, not water. You have no idea how beautiful it is here. You are all so lucky."

"Can you tell us a bit about Medar?" Tarek asked.

So far so good. "Sure. First of all, the whole land is covered in cloud. You never see the sun. The sky is not blue; it's grey. But I never knew any of that until I came to Tyrelia. The only reason I was able to get out of Medar and into Tyrelia was because I found a magical tablet that told me about Tyrelia and the Ancient. I believed in the Ancient and was able to pass through the Wall."

"Why don't all those other people in Medar just come here, too? Like you did?" Peregrine asked.

"They don't know about Tyrelia. Nobody's ever heard about the Ancient." The look of disbelief on their faces encouraged her. "Unless we go to Medar and tell people about the Ancient, they'll never get a chance to believe, let alone get through the Wall. They only believe in the Master there. They think he's good, but he's not. My family—" she swallowed a lump that threatened to choke her, "—are trapped in the Golden City. They received an injection that prevents them from leaving. But we've found the antidote. It's the water from the headwaters of the Helix River. Now we just need people to help us get it to them." She flung her hands out. "We need you."

During her impassioned speech, a small crowd had gathered. The eyes of ten people were fastened on her. She dropped her head. It was embarrassing having the attention of so many people.

"Look," Peregrine said, pointing at Freya.

It's my scar. Freya covered her eye and started turning away. The next words stopped her.

"What's that around her waist?" Peregrine continued.

"It just appeared," Tarek said, his eyes huge. "Like magic."

Freya's hands flew to her stomach. "By the Ancient!"

"The belt," Willow breathed.

And so it was. A wide leather belt encircled her waist. It was engraved with intricate markings that glinted in the sunlight and *glowed.*

Freya sucked in her breath and smiled at Nyx.

He chuckled, his eyes twinkling. "Well done, Freya. You've earned the belt. Your *'yes is your yes'*. I'm proud of you. And

Saff would be, too."

Heat flooded her cheeks. She felt lighter inside. "Thank you, Brother Nyx."

Tarek climbed onto the first tread. "I'm in," he declared, beaming.

A girl with long blonde hair stepped forward, dragging her friend with her. "We want to join the whatever-you-call-it, too. The Delfy."

Nyx beckoned them closer. "Tell me, what are your names and how old are you?"

The blonde spoke up. "My name's Diana. I'm seventeen."

"And I'm Amber," her friend supplied. "I'm seventeen too."

"Wonderful," Brother Nyx said. "Go ask your parents."

A plump middle-aged woman elbowed her way forwards. "I'm Diana's mother. I'd be absolutely honoured if you were to train my daughter in the lost traditions of the Adelphi. Honoured." She dipped her head.

"As would I," added a slender woman with auburn hair swept up in a bun. She gave a small curtsey. "I'm Amber's mother."

Nyx beamed around at the four, young people. "Well, that's settled then. We have enough recruits for now. Gather your things and come back here as soon as you can. You have much to learn."

~

The first task was to choose their stones. Peregrine chose the peridot stone and asked to be called Peri from then on. Tarek took the turquoise and the nickname 'Turq'. Amber—well, of course, she claimed the amber and kept her name. Diana chose the diamond and changed her name to Di. They mastered their stones that first day.

Now they were practising warping again. As he had done

with Freya and Willow, Nyx assembled all the acolytes near the Law Pillar.

"Can you sense the vibrations?" he asked, peering at them.

"Yes, of course," Amber said. She had long, wavy red hair and was the most outspoken of the new recruits.

"In a sense, we're going to travel on the vibrations. Imagine a sort of bridge of vibrations connecting the pillars."

Turq nodded, his brown skin the perfect canvas for his warm brown eyes and tight black curly hair. "Oh yeah, I can imagine that."

Peri frowned, his light brows drawn together. A fuzz of hair lined his upper lip and chin.

"Who's first?" Nyx asked.

Di sashayed forward, tossing her blonde head. "Can I, please?" She fluttered her eyelashes at Peri and Turq, who both grinned stupidly at her.

Freya, Willow and Alex rolled their eyes. "This is going to be fun," Alex muttered.

Amber shot him a glance. "Is it?" she asked eagerly.

"Oh, not really," Willow replied. "I almost threw up the first time I did it."

Amber's smile faded.

"But you get used to it," Freya encouraged her.

Nyx grasped Di's elbow and shuffled towards the Law Pillar.

"Oh," she yelped, as she disappeared. Within minutes, they were back. Di's face was pallid. She stumbled slightly when Nyx released her elbow.

"Who's next?" Nyx asked, peering around.

"I'll give it a go." Peri took a deep breath and stepped forward, wiping his palms on his trousers.

Before long, Nyx had warped them all individually to the

pillar near the Wastelands. "Right," he announced, "now it's time for you all to practise in pairs or threes."

Amber and Di paired up, as did Peri and Turq. Freya, Alex and Willow formed a trio. They practised warping for several hours. At the end of the day, they all trooped into the dining hall, exhausted but exhilarated, except Brother Nyx who retired to his chamber.

"That was *amazing*," said Amber.

Di nodded enthusiastically. "It sure was."

Willow buttered her bread intently.

Freya nudged her in the side. "Cheer up. You'll manage it soon."

Willow grunted. "I dunno. Even Alex has managed it. And I've been an acolyte longer than any of them. Except you." She sighed. "Maybe it's a sign that I should go back to tending sheep."

"Yeah, maybe you should," Amber called across the table. "You're that *baaad*." She shrieked with laughter at her own joke. The others joined in.

Willow's head snapped up, her green eyes flashing and her cheeks flushed. Pushing away from the table, she dashed from the room, chased by Amber's peals of laughter.

Chapter 11

THE SHADY DESERT

Thyst nestled deep into the bushes at the side of the track before allowing herself to become visible. She concentrated on the purple stone in her palm, and Rube's face materialised in the swirling glow. "Rube, where are you?" she asked urgently.

"I'm at the outskirts of Yawside. Where are you?"

"I'm at Little Farthing. So, you're just a bit further north than me."

"Where shall I meet you tomorrow morning?"

"As you approach the town from the south, there's a farm on the outskirts. Right at the back of it, there's a dovecot. I'll be concealed in the trees nearby."

"Good. As long as you don't need me to steal any eggs. That didn't go down too well last time." Thyst tried to smile, but it got tangled up with an unexpected lump in her throat and ended in a grimace. She'd been with Saff, a week or so after they'd seen Freya disappear through the Wall into Tyrelia. They'd split up to scavenge some food, and she'd nearly been caught helping herself to some eggs. The farmer's wife had, understandably, mistaken Thyst for a ghost. That incident had almost blown their cover. *Oh, Saff.*

Rube shook his head. "No, I'm good for now." He smiled gently. "See you soon."

~

Giving the farmhouse a wide berth, Thyst slid off Dapple and led her by the bridle. They might be invisible, but her horse could make a noise, especially if it sensed other animals. Ah, there was the dovecot. She picked her way towards it, sticking to the treeline, checking the farmhouse for movement. "Rube," she whispered. She paused and cocked her head. Peered into the trees. Nothing. She suppressed a snort. Of course she couldn't see anything: Rube was invisible too.

She was directly under the pole supporting the dovecot now. Abruptly, a pair of doves burst out of their nesting box, startling her horse. Dapple whinnied, shying backwards, tearing the reins out of Thyst's grasp. The animal became visible. "Dapple," Thyst cried, snatching at the reins.

"Thyst," Rube called.

Thyst spun, her hand to her chest. "Rube, there you are." Securing the reins, she turned Dapple invisible again and followed Rube into the copse, scanning behind her to ensure the farmers hadn't been alerted. All was quiet.

Once they were well into the forest, Rube appeared.

Thyst released Dapple and ran to him. She hugged him tightly. Oh, it was so good to see another Watcher again. A lump rose in her throat, and she blinked away tears.

Rube patted her back. "There, there, my dear," he soothed.

Thyst stumbled backwards, brushing her sleeve across her eyes. "It's just you and me, now," she said.

Rube gripped her shoulders. "Yes, but not for too much longer. This time tomorrow, we should be meeting Brother Nyx at the obelisk. Now *that* was something I never anticipated. Meeting the Leader of the Adelphi."

"Yes, and Freya, too," Thyst said, her voice catching. "*Especially* Freya."

~

They plodded and plodded, the shifting sand soft underfoot, the grains sliding back into the hollows made by their horses' hooves, erasing all evidence of their passage. Thyst screwed up her eyes. "I've lost complete track of direction in this nothingness. How do you know we're going the right way?"

Rube gestured with his hand. "According to the map, the obelisk is roughly half a day's travel north-west of Yawside."

Thyst nodded. "Yes, that's what Brother Nyx said. But how do you know we're on the right bearing?"

"Well, I've been keeping an eye on the sun—as best as I can tell, obscured as it is by all that cloud. See, it's a bit brighter there, so due north is that way and we need to travel that way." He pointed. "But I've never been there myself."

On and on they trudged.

After a while, Rube reined in Cirrus. "Can you see the obelisk, Thyst?" he asked, peering about him.

Thyst shook her head, her curls tickling her face. She scrutinised her surroundings.

Rube sighed. "I really don't want to keep going. We could end up wandering around here forever."

"What are we going to do?" Thyst asked.

"I'm going to call Brother Nyx. Maybe he'll have an idea." He pulled out his stone, and soon Nyx swirled in the shifting red hues.

"Brother Rube. What's wrong?"

"Well, I'm here in the Shady Desert with Thyst—"

Nyx's eyebrows shot up.

"—and we can't find the obelisk. Any suggestions?"

Nyx furrowed his brow, thinking. After a moment, he

cleared his throat. "Alright, here's what we're going to do …"

~

Thyst and Rube scanned the horizon, turning slowly on the spot, mounted on their horses.

"There." Thyst pointed.

Rube followed the direction of her outstretched arm and saw it too: a light in the distance, pulsing brightly.

Using her stone, Thyst returned several bursts of purple light. Then she focused her thoughts. "We're coming, Brother Nyx," she told him. "See you soon."

Soon, the murky outline of the obelisk loomed into sight. Minutes later, and the shape was clearly defined. Thyst shot off another burst of light. An answering flash came from the right-hand side of the obelisk. Thyst urged Dapple into a trot and Rube followed suit. There. Two figures.

Thyst leapt from her saddle and ran to Freya, enveloping her in a hug.

Rube greeted Brother Nyx.

"I'm so sorry, Thyst," Freya sobbed.

"Hush, Freya. It's not your fault," Thyst soothed, smoothing back Freya's fringe. "Saff would have wanted us both to be safe."

Thyst stepped back to allow Rube to greet Freya.

Freya smiled at him shyly. "Hello … Father."

Rube flushed. "Freya. Daughter. It's good to finally see you again." He hugged her tightly.

"When did you see each other last?" Brother Nyx asked.

"Yawbridge," Freya said.

"Yes, at my house, in fact," Rube said.

"Right before we all set off to the Andoria Mountains, except for Rube, who went off on his secret mission and wouldn't tell us what it was," Freya added.

"I had my suspicions that Freya was my natural daughter, but I didn't know for sure until I was able to talk to Freya's family in the Golden City," Rube explained. "And I've been there ever since. Except for now, of course. When Thyst told me that she was going to meet up with you both, I couldn't miss the opportunity."

"Plus, I wasn't entirely sure where the obelisk was," Thyst chipped in.

Nyx grunted. "Doesn't look like Rube was too much help in that area," he observed dryly.

Rube gave a tiny shake of his head, a smile playing on his lips. "Yeah, okay. I know."

"Anyhow, here's the water," Nyx said, producing a waterskin from some hidden pocket. He handed it to Rube.

"You'd better give it to Thyst," Rube said, rubbing his hip. "She's more agile than I am."

Thyst chuckled, arching a brow. She took the waterskin and tucked it away.

"One more thing," Rube said. He turned to rummage in a saddle bag. He pulled out a large, bulky, rectangular object, wrapped in paper.

"What's that?" Nyx asked.

"This," Rube said with a flourish, handing it to Freya, "Is the book I … ah … *borrowed* from the Master's library."

"The book about Tyrelia," Freya exclaimed.

"Yes. It's how we were able to figure out that water from the River Helix is the antidote to the injection. It needs to be kept safe. I can't think of anywhere safer than in Tyrelia itself," Rube said.

Freya hugged it to her chest. "I'll guard it with my life," she said solemnly.

Suddenly, a shape leapt at Freya.

"Look out!" Thyst yelled.

Freya spun as a gnome grabbed her around the neck, and she sprawled to the ground, the book spilling out of her grasp.

In a flash, Thyst nocked an arrow.

Rube lunged, grabbed the book, and turned himself invisible.

Nyx was nowhere to be seen.

Freya rolled on the ground, grappling with the gnome. "Help me," she gasped.

Abruptly, the gnome went limp, a dagger protruding from his back. Nyx materialised beside it.

Freya pushed the gnome off and scrabbled to her feet.

Rube thrust the book into her hands. "Quick. You need to get out of here," he commanded.

Nyx laid his hand on Freya's arm and, in an instant, they were gone.

"There are more coming," Thyst said urgently. She ran to Dapple and leapt up into the saddle.

Rube limped to Cirrus.

He was too slow. "Make yourself invisible, Rube," she hissed. "I'll cover you."

Two more gnomes emerged from behind the obelisk, the first was immediately struck down by an arrow. The other stopped in his tracks, his eyes darting, searching for the archer.

But there was no sign of any foe. Just the desert sands, stretching to the horizon. And some hoof tracks, leading away. Within minutes, they too had melted into the sand.

Chapter 12

LEVEL TWO GAMES

Level Two was as good as Jack had imagined. He'd had to change trades, of course. No farming jobs up here. Now, thanks to his association with Straw and Hay, he was an apprentice blacksmith. He flexed his bicep and admired the bulge. It had only been a week, but he was looking toned already.

Being stronger would undoubtedly help with his wrestling, too. Talking of which, they needed to get moving. "Hey, guys," he called from the kitchen, "are you ready to go? Games start in less than an hour and we need to warm up and check out our competitors."

"Coming." Straw emerged pulling his shirt over his head. Hay followed. Straw patted the basket on the kitchen table. "Aw, you've packed our lunches already? Thanks, man."

"Yeah, and your breakfast's over there." Jack nodded towards the bench. "I picked up rations for you both, too." His gaze lingered on the pile of dirty plates and cups he'd hastily stacked next to the sink. These guys were such slobs. No time to clean up now though.

Minutes later, the three young men were sauntering down the road. The paved boulevard was flanked by tidy, whitewashed cottages sporting pots of red geraniums on their window-sills. The few citizens out and about this early greeted them with a cheery wave. Everyone loved games day—their one day off a week. The scent of freshly baked bread wafted from a bakery. It all felt strangely familiar—yes, they were in a new level, but it was set out the same as Level One: the rations warehouse was located adjacent to the gate, just like in Level One. The well was right outside that—just like in Level One. The Games Arena was at the end of the street—just like Level One. Jack half expected to see Ma waiting for him inside the stadium. He shook the thought away with a toss of his head.

Once inside, they headed to the wrestling ring. The layout inside the arena was also identical to Level One. Freaky. Their new trainer, Joe, leaned against the ropes, his arms folded. Jack hailed him as he hurried forward. "Hi Joe."

"You made it. Good, good. Join the rest of the team warming up." Joe pointed to the line of men jogging around the perimeter.

After completing a series of lunges, jumps and stretches, they gathered around Joe, panting. Sweat dribbled down their faces and dripped off their chins. "Listen up, lads. Here's the draw." Joe reeled off their names and who they'd be competing against.

Fortunately, Jack wouldn't have to face Straw or Hay, as they were much heavier and in a different weight class. He eyed up his opponent: similar height and build. Fair hair: thick and curly. Covered half his face, too. Peter was his name. Because this was Jack's first match in Level Two, he was back to being an 'uncrowned wrestler', even though he'd won multiple times in the Level One games. It also meant that his match was first up. That sucked. He wouldn't get a chance to see his opponent in action before they fought.

Joe beckoned him over. "Are you ready Jack? In you go."

Jack and Peter shook hands with the referee, then faced each other in the neutral position. The referee blew his whistle.

Jack scowled at his opponent. He reached out to grip Peter's shoulder. Peter swatted his hand away and grabbed Jack's shoulder instead. Jack wrapped his arm around Peter's, and they circled, locked together. Jack flicked his other hand out, attempting to get purchase on Peter's arm or leg. But Peter's limbs evaded him. Peter pushed his head into Jack's. Next thing, Jack's head was down, and he dropped to a knee. He released Peter and danced backwards, barely missing the boundary line.

Peter lunged and once again they were locked up. Without warning, Jack was on his knees, the other man's arms wrapped around his waist, pushing him backwards.

"Go Jack!" a kid yelled. The voice sounded vaguely familiar.

Jack grunted. He braced himself and gave an almighty shove, twisting as he did so. Somehow, he managed to flip Peter over. Now Jack was lying on his back on top of him. But he couldn't keep him pinned down. Peter rolled from under him.

"Good stuff, Jack. Keep it up," Joe called.

Jack and Peter circled each other once more, reaching out, grabbing, pushing, testing each other's strength. Peter went down on one knee and yanked Jack's ankle. He was falling. Jack lunged, landing on top of Peter and grabbed his ankle. They spun, locked together like two crabs. They flipped, and Jack's breath whooshed from his lungs. The whistle blew. Jack's foot had gone out of bounds. Peter had won the round.

Jack lay there, gasping. He staggered to his feet and stumbled over to Joe. Straw clapped him on the shoulder. "You're doing great, Jack," he encouraged.

Joe thrust a cup of water into his hands. "Drink up."

"What's the score?" Jack asked, after he'd taken a swig.

"Four to Peter, three to you. It's close. You can take him, Jack. Off you go." Joe pushed him back into the ring.

The next two rounds were a blur of grabbing limbs, pushing, pulling, flipping and spinning. Leg sweeps, escapes, reversals, and near falls. The points racked up, Peter staying ahead. Just. The bout finished with one point in it.

Jack dropped onto the stool, dripping with sweat. He gulped some water.

Joe slapped him on the back. "Very nice, Jack. I can see you're going to make me some good money." He turned away. "Fred," he called, "you're up."

Wearily, Jack dragged himself to the bleachers, where he flopped down next to Straw.

A hand patted him on the shoulder from behind, and a young boy said, "Well done, Jack, you were amazing."

Jack twisted. "Sam," he said. "What are you doing here?" His eyes swept over the bleachers. "Are you here by yourself?"

"No. Me ma and da are here too." The young lad gestured higher up the bleachers to his left. By the Master, Leena and Hank were indeed there. Jack raised a hand and they waved back.

"Is my ma here, too?" Jack asked, his heart skipping a beat. He scanned the people surrounding Hank and Leena.

"Nah, she's still in Level One," Sam said.

"What are you all doing here?" Jack asked.

The boy shrugged. "I dunno. The Guards made us come, but I don't mind. You should ask my parents."

Following Sam up the bleachers, Jack approached Hank and Leena warily, painfully aware that the last time he'd seen them had been when he'd taken the Guards to their house in the middle of the night to arrest Rube. "Hello Hank, Leena … ma'am," he said. He shook Hank's hand. "How … what are you doing here?"

Leena cocked her head to one side. "Why, we're watching you wrestle, Jack. I don't know much about it, but you seemed to handle yourself well?"

Jack jerked his chin. "Yeah, I did okay. I lost, though."

Hank clapped his shoulder. "You did fine, lad. Your da would be proud."

Jack felt his face grow warm. That was awkward. He studied his feet. Out of the corner of his eye, he saw Leena swat Hank's arm.

Hank coloured. He rubbed his stubble. "Apparently a printer in another level has passed on, so we all got moved up." He fixed Jack with a stare. "We didn't have a choice, unlike some."

"Oh," Jack said. He shoved his hands in his pockets. "I'm sorry about … you know," he mumbled.

Leena sighed. "Yes, well. It wasn't a particularly smart decision, Jack. But here we all are, still in one piece. And just so you know, your ma will be fine."

So, Rube was still with her then. That was just as well. He shuffled his feet. "It was nice seeing you again." He turned away.

Leena reached out a hand and caught his singlet. "Jack," she said. "None of us know many people here. We may as well put that … *incident* … in the past. Look for us after the games and we'll show you where we live. You can have dinner with us."

Jack gave a small smile. "Thanks, Leena. I will." He mock-tipped a hat to Hank. "Bye, Hank. See you later, Sam."

He bounded back down the bleachers to his friends, feeling lighter, somehow.

Chapter 13

AN ACCIDENTAL DISCOVERY

Thyst and Rube crept beside the moat towards the drawbridge. They'd left the horses hidden in a copse and had spent the past hour on foot. The white walls of the Golden City gleamed dully in the early morning light.

"It's beautiful," Thyst whispered.

"A beautiful trap," Rube retorted. "It may promise to be gold, but it's really an icy net. Now, the trick will be to get across the bridge, past the guard room and through the archways without making a noise. We'll wait until after the farmers come out, and then we'll slip in. When you get through the archways, turn right and wait for me next to the wall."

"Okay."

Before long, a muffled tramping sound throbbed on the air. A subdued group of about forty people trooped across the bridge behind four Guards, who fingered whips tucked into their belts. Four more Guards brought up the rear. Thyst observed them with disgust, taking in their pallid grey skin and dull eyes.

Rube squeezed her arm. "Let's go," he whispered.

She waited a heartbeat, then stepped onto the drawbridge

and tiptoed across. Thank the Land for the cloud cover, which meant they weren't casting any shadows. As she entered the gloom under the gateway, she gazed curiously about. To her right was an ordinary-looking timber door, but it was the series of archways ahead that caught her attention. Each opening was large enough to admit only one person at a time. She crept forward. Tiny red lights lined the lintel. *What were they for?* She held her breath as she passed. Nothing happened. She let out the breath. *Turn right and wait by the wall.* She reached out a hand and touched the whitewashed wall. It was cool. "Rube?" she whispered.

"I'm here."

An invisible hand brushed her arm. Rube grasped her elbow. "I'll take you to Martha's house. She won't be home, but we should be safe there."

They set off.

~

Martha let herself wearily into her house. It had been another tiring day. Rube materialised.

"Rube," she yelped, her hand flying to her heart.

Rube gave her a peck on the cheek. "Martha, I have someone I'd like you to meet. Thyst, you can show yourself."

Instantly, Thyst materialised, seated at the other end of the table. She rose and took two quick steps towards Martha. "Greetings, Martha. I'm so pleased to finally meet you."

Martha smiled and hugged the Watcher. "Thyst. Likewise, it's a pleasure. How long have you both been here? Did you see Freya?" The words tumbled out.

"Since right after you left this morning." Rube beamed. "And yes, she's fine."

"So, you got the water, then?" Hope bloomed in her chest.

"Yes, we did," Thyst replied. She reached inside her robes

and produced a waterskin. She laid it on the table. "Here it is."

"What we don't know is the dosage," Rube declared. He sighed. "We do know that it's mighty potent. Freya went into a coma when she drank some, and she has Tyrelian blood. We have no idea what impact it might have on someone with *no* Tyrelian blood."

Martha's mouth went dry. "Perhaps if we dilute it in *normal* water?"

Thyst nodded. "That's not a bad idea."

"I agree," Rube said. "If you could be so kind as to get a cup, Martha?"

She took one from the cupboard and placed it on the table. Then she picked up the water urn from the corner of the room. "Oh dear," she said.

"What's wrong?" Thyst asked.

"I'm completely out of water," Martha said. "I'm going to have to draw more from the well." She glanced out the window. It was starting to get dark. "I'll be as quick as I can."

"We'll come with you," Rube said. "Just in case. And it'll give Thyst a chance to see a bit more of the City."

Martha nodded.

They went out the back door, so it wasn't obvious when it stayed open longer than it should have for one person exiting their house. Or that it closed by itself.

Martha swung the urn onto her head. She smiled at the Guard stationed opposite her house. "Good evening," she called. That was dumb. She'd probably drawn attention to herself. Or maybe she'd distract him from noticing any additional noises. She hoped the latter. She turned right, then left. There it was.

She set her urn down on the ground beside the well. A bucket rested on the edge of the stonework. She pushed it off.

It swung into the cavity, clattering as it hit the other side.

"Hello love," said a gruff voice.

The Guard had followed her. He moved into her space, pressing his face towards her. "Oh!" she gasped.

"How about a kiss, then?" he demanded. "You must be missing that, with your husband gone." He smirked and reached for her.

She swerved sideways and bumped into an invisible person. She recovered her footing and ran away from the well. She faced the Guard once more. "Please, Sir. Don't."

"Don't what?" He leered at her and leaned back against the well.

Splash!

The Guard's eyes went wide, and he spun towards the well. "What was that?" he demanded.

Martha feigned innocence. "What was what?"

"That splash. And I felt something on my back," the Guard growled.

Martha jutted her chin. "That would be the bucket hitting the water."

The Guard gripped the bricks and checked the well. "What the? By the Master. There's something in there."

Suddenly, the Guard jerked backwards and flung himself to the ground. Or rather, *someone* flung him to the ground. His face snapped sideways as he was punched in the jaw. He sighed and lay still.

Rube materialised beside him, rubbing his fist. "Ouch. That hurt," he said. Then he ran to the well and bent over the edge. "Thyst, Thyst! Are you all right?" he called.

A hollow splashing was followed by an echoey response. "Yes, I think so. Can you help me out? Wind up the rope."

Rube grabbed the winch and tried turning it. He grunted

with exertion.

Martha ran over, skirting the unconscious Guard. "Let me help."

Straining together, they slowly wound the winch up.

Eventually, Thyst's bedraggled head came into sight. She reached up, grabbed the lip of the well and heaved herself onto the edge. She was soaking wet. Water dripped off the tip of her nose and off the ends of her lank hair. A pool of water formed around her. She grabbed a handful of her robes and wrung them out.

The Guard moaned.

"Quick, we need to fill that jar with water," Rube said.

"Let me," Martha said. She'd done this a hundred times before. She pushed the bucket back into the well and let the handle free-wheel. As soon as the bucket had sunk below the surface of the water, she wound it up. With a smooth motion, she swung it over the edge and tipped the contents into her urn. "Let's go," she said. Placing the urn on top of her head, she hurried back home.

Once inside, she placed the urn on the floor. She let out a deep breath. "Oh my. That was close," she said. Thyst appeared. "Thyst. Let's get you out of those wet things. Follow me."

She marched into the bathroom and handed Thyst a towel. "Wait here," she said. She flung her wardrobe door open and selected a dress. Then she opened a drawer and grabbed some stockings and underwear. She'd only have one change left for herself now. *Too bad.* She hurried back to the bathroom with the dry clothes and left Thyst to change.

Soon after, Thyst joined them in the kitchen, much drier, but clearly stricken.

"What's wrong?" Rube demanded.

Thyst held out a black limp thing. It was the waterskin. "It's empty," she said morosely. "It must've emptied in the well. The stopper's gone. I'm so sorry, Martha," she wailed.

Rube's jaw dropped open. Then he snapped his mouth shut. His Adam's apple bobbed. "That's too bad, Thyst," he said. He clenched his teeth. "Well, there's nothing for it. We'll just have to get another pouch." He placed a hand over Martha's. "We will get you and Thomas out of this city, Martha. I promise."

~

The next morning, an invisible Thyst and Rube trailed out of the City behind the farmers. As soon as they had crossed the drawbridge, they peeled off to the left, striking towards the bushes where Rube had concealed himself outside the gates. They had not gone far, however, when they heard shouts and screams from the farmers.

"What's going on?" Thyst asked.

"I don't know," Rube responded. "Let's go and find out."

They headed towards the noise. They soon saw what was causing the uproar. One of the oxen was charging here and there, chasing down farmers, who were scattering in all directions.

The beast set its sights on one particular young man. It lowered its head and charged. The man yelped and zig-zagged away, hoping to confuse the animal. The Guards stood off to the sides, watching the events unfold, making no attempt to intervene.

"Oh no," Rube muttered under his breath.

"What?" Thyst asked.

"That man is too close to the boundary," Rube said.

"What boundary?" she asked, squinting.

"The distance that binds the inhabitants of the Golden City," Rube explained. "The injection only allows them to go so far outside the City. Any further and ..." He made a choking sound.

Thyst glanced to her left, but Rube was invisible. "Are you all right?" she asked.

"Oh, yes. I forgot you couldn't see me. I mean they die."

"Right," Thyst murmured.

At that very moment, one of the fleeing farmers collapsed to his knees, then fell to the ground, spasms convulsing his body. But another ran straight past the dying farmer.

"By the Land," Rube said.

The other people who'd scattered beyond the boundary were now running away from the City. Hard.

Some of the Guards, whips in hand, gave chase. But there were too many fleeing in too many different directions. Another group of farmers stood and stared at the ones escaping, muttering to each other in hushed voices.

One of the Guards issued a piercing whistle, causing his comrades to stop in their tracks. Thyst couldn't hear what he said, but the Guards gave up the chase and returned to the group. Before long, the Guards were herding the farmers back towards the City.

"Quick," Rube whispered. "Let's get into the City before them."

~

Back at the house, Rube, Thyst and Martha conferred in low voices.

"I think," Rube hypothesised, "that we've discovered the correct dose of Helix water. We diluted a single pouch of Helix water into the Level One well. I'll guarantee you, those farmers that escaped had a drink of well-water this morning."

Thyst beamed at him and clasped Martha's hand. "It would seem so. Praise the Land."

"So, what now?" Martha asked.

"Good question," Rube said. "We need to get a cup of that water to Thomas, so we can get you both out of the City. Then, we need to inform Brother Nyx of this development."

They beamed at each other. "Let's do it," Thyst said.

Chapter 14

INVISIBILITY

Lined up on the grass with her fellow acolytes, Freya was mesmerised by Brother Nyx swaying on the top step.

"Today I will teach you how to turn yourselves invisible," Nyx announced.

A murmur of anticipation rippled through them. "At last," Freya said under her breath. She shot a glance at Willow, who had joined the very end of the row—as far from Amber as she could get, Freya noted.

"All Tyrelians, whether by birth or by choice—" Brother Nyx fluttered a hand in Freya's direction, "—have the ability to turn themselves invisible due to the powers you inherited from drinking the waters of the Helix River. It is one of the many gifts that the Ancient has bestowed on those of us lucky enough to live in Tyrelia. All you need to do is accept this free gift for yourself."

Willow squeezed Freya's hand.

"Close your eyes," he said. "Now, reach out with your senses. Can you feel the vibrations in the air?"

Freya *mm'd* and nodded her head. She sensed Willow doing the same.

"Good, good. Now, imagine those vibrations are in harmony with your own heart beat."

Freya focussed on the rhythmic beating of her heart. Gradually, her pulse grew louder, until it drummed in her ears.

"Allow the vibration to embrace you."

Freya concentrated, her eyes still shut tight, straining to hear Nyx's voice. Why was he speaking so quietly?

"Well done, everyone. Open your eyes."

"How did we do?" Freya asked.

"Some of you did better than others," Nyx admitted. "Peri, Turq, Amber and Di managed to disappear completely." He beamed at them. "Freya, you started to go transparent. I'm afraid Willow and Alex remained quite solid, though."

Peri and Turq high-fived each other. Amber flipped her long red hair over her shoulder, looking smug. Di lifted her chin, smiling serenely. "It wasn't very difficult," she said.

"*It wasn't very difficult,*" Willow mimicked under her breath. Alex snorted.

"What did you say?" Di demanded, stepping around Alex to glare at Willow.

Nyx thumped his staff on the marble steps. "Quiet! Get back in line, please. Now, let's try again. Close your eyes. You too, Willow. Concentrate."

Once more, all other sounds receded as the rhythm of Freya's blood filled her senses: a steady *thump, thump, thump*.

"Good, Peri," Brother Nyx murmured. Then, "Yes, well done, Amber. Yes, Di and Turq. Keep it up, all of you."

Willow huffed. "It's not working."

Down the line, Amber piped up. "Probably because you're a Betan. That's why we Henevans are *beatin'* you."

Peri, Di and Turq laughed. "Good one, Amber," Di giggled.

Freya's eyes popped open and she craned her neck.

"Oh, shut up." Alex retorted, rounding on Di who was standing closest to him.

Nyx thumped his staff on the steps. "Acolytes, this is not a competition. I did not realise it would be this tiresome, training up new Adelphi." He scowled at them. "Try again, please."

Once more, they all closed their eyes and concentrated on their heartbeats. Freya couldn't resist. She cracked her eye open and glanced down at herself. Huh, she wasn't completely invisible, but she wasn't completely visible either. She took a peek at Willow. She was still completely solid.

"Oh, this is so easy," floated Amber's voice from the other end.

Willow spun. "Excuse me," she blurted, and she dashed off towards the forest.

"Willow," Freya called.

Willow kept running, dodging through the trees. Freya took off, hot on her heels.

Sobbing, Willow flung herself at the base of a tree.

Freya dropped to her knees beside her. She patted Willow's back, then drew her into a hug. "Don't cry," she said, rocking Willow gently.

Willow sniffled against Freya's shoulder.

Freya pressed a handkerchief into Willow's hand.

Willow dabbed at her eyes. She pulled away from Freya and blew her nose. "I can't do it, Freya," she said in a small voice. "I'm a failure. Why can't I turn myself invisible?"

Freya sat back on her heels and tilted her head. "Turn yourself invisible?" she repeated. "That's it." She snapped her fingers.

Willow glanced up. "Huh?"

"You can't turn yourself invisible," Freya said. "And neither can I."

Willow massaged her temple. "What are you going on about? Of course you can turn yourself invisible."

Freya shook her head. "No, Willow, I can't." She threw her arms wide, as if embracing the world. "It's the Ancient who turns us invisible. Not us."

Willow's eyes widened. "Oh."

Freya nodded, smiling. "We don't have any special powers of our own. We just need to learn to tap into the Ancient's power."

Willow sniffed. "I guess I'll give it another try."

"Let's try now," Freya suggested. She sat down opposite Willow, legs crossed. "Close your eyes and think of the Ancient."

Willow did as instructed.

"Wow," Freya said.

"What?"

"Open your eyes, Willow. Look at yourself."

Willow whooped. "I did it. I mean, the Ancient did it!" She became visible again.

Freya grinned. "Nice one. Ready to go back to the others?"

Willow sighed. "I suppose. I just wish Amber would shut up."

"Yeah, well, Amber's a bully."

"What would you know about bullies? You're *amazing*. You figured out how to get out of Medar—the first person in a thousand years. And you're *the One*—earning the pieces of the Tyrelian Armour."

"You may think I'm amazing. But until I discovered that tablet, I was a nobody. Worse than a nobody. I was an outcast."

"But why?"

Freya swept her hair back from her face, exposing her scar and blind eye. "Because of this. I've been bullied about it my whole life."

"Pah," Willow said. "That's dumb. Why would someone bully you for what you look like? That's got *nothing* to do with your abilities."

Freya shrugged. "Maybe that's how people think here, in Tyrelia. But not in Medar. People value completely different things, there."

"Obviously."

Freya stood up and held out a hand to Willow. "Let's work on you not giving up. Ignore Amber," she said. "You can't control how she behaves. But you *can* control how you behave."

Willow held her arm up. "You're right, of course." She groaned as Freya hauled her to her feet. "Thanks, Freya. You're a good friend."

"Sure thing. Let's get back to the others."

As they emerged from the trees, Amber turned to look at them. "Oh, she came back. I don't know why she bothered."

Freya marched up to her, barely registering Nyx hobbling towards them. "What is your problem?" she demanded.

Amber smirked. "Willow's my problem. She's useless. She should be everyone's problem."

Freya folded her arms across her chest. "Actually, Amber, you're the problem. We're Adelphi. We're a team. We need to be able to trust each other *completely*. I know if I had to choose between you and Willow to go into battle with … I'd choose Willow any day. So now *you* need to make a choice. Either you stay and start acting like an Adelphi, or you go back to Heneva."

Amber gaped at Freya.

The others all looked stunned too.

"What?" Freya asked. "Hasn't anyone stood up to you

before?"

Behind her, Willow said, "It's not that, Freya. Look at yourself. You've just earned the breastplate."

Freya's hands flew to her chest. By the Ancient. So she had.

~

The City loomed before her; her army was massed at her back. She brandished her sword in the air and yelled, "Onwards!" They surged forwards, she on her white steed. The gates burst open and an enormous black snake slithered out to meet them. No, not a snake. A column of Guards. As they neared, they resolved into individuals, armed with spears and swords. They engaged, and she leaned down from her saddle, slashing and thrusting her sword. She missed. Why hadn't she learned swordplay? A Guard stabbed his blade into her foot. That's right, she hadn't earned the shoes yet. Watch out! someone yelled. She looked up just in time to see the flaming arrow bearing down on her. She flung her shield up, but she hadn't learnt how to use that either. Why, oh why, hadn't she learned how to fight?

Chapter 15

CONSPIRACY

It was risky attempting an escape during daylight hours, but the farmers had been banned from working outside the City for the rest of the day, so it was a prime opportunity. One they couldn't afford to miss. That was Rube's thinking, anyhow.

It was good having Thyst to help him, too. He would never get both Thomas and Martha out without her help. He checked behind him but, of course, he couldn't see either Thyst or Martha. He angled for the printhouse, ducking in and out of shadows, sticking close to the wall. A troupe of Guards marched past. The second one they'd seen. The Guards were obviously nervous about what had happened outside the City. And rightly so. What must they be thinking? Would the Master figure out how the farmers were able to escape? Another reason to make haste.

He sidled up to a corner and poked his head around. A Guard was leaning against the wall, right there. Rube pulled back, holding his breath. At that moment, Thyst bumped into him.

"Ouch," she yelped.

The Guard leaped into the street. "Who's there?" he

demanded, flicking his head from side to side.

They all froze, flattening themselves against the wall.

The Guard had a black eye and a puffy nose. Drat. It was the one he'd thumped. The man gave a grunt of frustration and marched off down the street.

"That was close," Rube said.

"Was that ...?" Martha ventured.

"Yes, the one from the well. We need to hurry." They rounded the corner and there, opposite, was the printing warehouse.

Thyst allowed Martha to become visible.

Martha crossed the street and knocked on the door. Rube and Thyst, both invisible, followed her.

A worker opened the door. "Yes?" he asked.

"Oh, hello," Martha said brightly. "I knew Hank. I was wondering if I could meet the new printer?"

"Yes, Ma'am, I remember you. Sure, come on in." The man moved back to let Martha pass.

She paused after entering, allowing time for her eyes to adjust to the dim interior, and to let Rube and Thyst to follow her. Rube smiled as he crept past her. She was doing well. The familiar smell of ink and parchment assailed his nostrils.

"Follow me, please," the man said. He led Martha down the main aisle between two massive printing presses. The man knocked on the door at the far end of the room.

"Enter," said a voice from within.

The man opened the door and ushered Martha inside.

A man behind the desk looked up with surprise. He stood, his chair scraping the floor. "Hello, Madam. How can I be of assistance?" he asked, bowing slightly.

Martha sailed into the room, her hand extended. "Good sir, I'm delighted to meet you. My name is Martha. I knew the previous printer."

The man paused. "Oh, is that so?" He beamed. "The name's Hanson. What can I do for you?"

Martha glanced behind her where the other man was still holding the door open. She lowered her voice and leaned towards the printer. "May we speak in private, please Sir?"

The printer's mouth twitched. He nodded at the other man. "Taylor, close the door, will you?" He gestured to the chair opposite his desk. "Please, take a seat. Now, how can I help you?"

Martha sat very straight and folded her hands in her lap. "Did you hear about what happened to the farmers outside the City today?" she asked.

Hanson's eyes went wide. "Yes, as a matter of fact. I understand there's some sort of sickness that's going around — highly contagious, it is. A whole bunch of farmers have died. I've been instructed to print this quarantine notice." He placed his hand on a poster on his desk.

Rube snorted. He couldn't help himself.

Hanson's head jerked up. He looked suspiciously around the room.

Martha clapped her hands together to mask the sound. "Hanson, there is no contagious sickness amongst the farmers. They didn't die. They escaped." She held her breath and waited for his reaction.

A range of emotions crossed his features: surprise followed by hope, then suspicion. "How do you know this?" he asked in a low voice.

Martha leaned towards him. "Because I'm a farmer. I was there. I saw it with my own eyes."

Hanson sat back, holding on to the desk. "But … how is that possible?" he asked. "The injection …"

Martha nodded. "I know. It should be impossible. Yet … there many things in this world that should be impossible."

Hanson frowned. "What are you talking about?"

Without taking her eyes off Hanson, Martha said, "Rube. Show yourself."

Rube materialised.

Hanson jumped with fright and almost fell off his chair. "By the Master," he exclaimed loudly.

"Hush," Rube said. "I'm sorry for frightening you, but there was no other way. Martha speaks the truth. The farmers escaped."

"Who—who are you?" Hanson stammered. "How did you do that?"

Rube smiled, aiming for a friendly look. "My name is Rube, and I'm a Watcher. My ancestors came from a place called Tyrelia, and the gift of invisibility runs in our veins."

Hanson gaped. "Never heard of Tyrelia." He narrowed his eyes. "Watcher, you say. Never heard of that either. But aren't you that Transient fellow?" He rifled through a pile of papers on his desk. "I knew it," he said triumphantly, whipping out the WANTED poster of Rube. He gave a low whistle. "Ten thousand units."

Rube held his hands out. "Don't make any rash decisions. I know ten thousand units is a lot of money—"

"Too right it is," Hanson muttered.

"—but what if I told you that I can get you out of the Golden City? Isn't that worth more than ten thousand units?" Rube asked.

Hanson cocked his head to one side, considering.

Rube held his breath.

Hanson leaned forward. "Would you be able to get my family out, too? I have a wife and two daughters."

Rube exhaled. He nodded. "Yes. Yes, I would."

"Alright then. I won't tell the Guards about you. So, how do we get out?"

"Can I sit down?" Rube asked. "This is going to take a bit of explaining."

"Of course."

Martha moved to the next chair and Rube settled in to the one she'd vacated. He flicked a smile at the corner of the room. That was the signal for Thyst to lower her bow and arrow, which Rube knew she would be aiming at Hanson's heart in case he made the wrong choice. Rube coughed and contemplated the printer. *Where to start?* "It would be one thing to get you out of the Golden City. It would be another to get you out of Medar entirely," Rube stated.

Hanson knitted his brow. "Out of Medar? How? To where?"

"Beyond the Wall is a land called Tyrelia. Where my ancestors are from. Tell me, Hanson, did you ever hear about the Visions?"

Hanson nodded slowly. "Sure. I know about them."

"Well, it's coming true. As we speak. The Girl in the Vision has been found. She's going to free the people of Medar from the Master's rule. She's figured out how to get through the Wall."

"By the Master," Hanson breathed.

Rube smiled. "We've also discovered the antidote to the injection."

Hanson gasped. "An antidote? Where is it? Can I have some?"

Rube shot a look at Martha before responding. They couldn't risk Hanson trying to leave the City before they were ready. "We need to get some more from Tyrelia. Hanson, we want to free *everyone* from the Golden City. Will you help us?"

Hanson's jaw dropped. "What could I possibly do?"

Rube raised his chin. "You could help spread the word; make sure that people are prepared for when the Girl comes."

A slow smile spread across Hanson's face. "A conspiracy," he said. He steepled his fingers under his chin. "I like it."

"Good." Rube nodded. "It's settled then. Now, there's one more thing."

"What's that, then?"

"We need to relieve you of your hidden guest."

"My what?"

Martha piped up. "Hank—your predecessor—was hiding my husband here."

"Here?" he asked bewildered, surveying the small room.

Martha stood up. "Yes. Let me show you." She edged past Rube to the filing cabinet behind Hanson. She slid her hand behind it. About half-way down, a faint *click* sounded. The cabinet swung forwards, revealing a door.

Hanson gripped the arms of his chair. "Well, I'll be ..."

She tapped out five quick knocks before opening the door. "Thomas," she called. "It's me. We've come to take you out."

"Martha?" Footsteps sounded and Thomas emerged. He stopped short when he spied Hanson.

"He's alright," Rube reassured him. "We've told him everything." Well, almost everything.

Thomas looked around the room, blinking like an owl.

Martha embraced him, then gestured. "Thomas, this is Hanson. Hanson, Thomas."

Hanson rose, gaping at Thomas. "Why ...?"

Martha sighed. "It's a long story. I'm sorry, but we really don't have time to tell it to you right now. Needless to say, *no one* can know that he was here."

"Well, it's going to be a bit difficult to keep it quiet once he walks out that door," Hanson said.

Rube stepped towards Thomas. "Actually, it's not." He clapped a hand on Thomas's shoulder, instantly turning them invisible.

Hanson stumbled backwards and fell into his chair. "By the Master."

The pair materialised once more. Rube smiled apologetically. "It's a lot to take in. But now we really must be leaving. We'll come back as soon as we can." Rube held out his hand to Hanson.

Hanson eyed it warily.

Rube chuckled. "It's safe. I won't turn you invisible."

Hanson shook Rube's hand, his face white.

"Remember, let people you trust know about the impending freedom."

Hanson nodded. "I will."

"Now, if you'd be so kind as to show Martha out, we'd be much obliged."

"Wait," Hanson said.

Rube paused.

"When will you come back?"

"All going to plan, in about eight days," Rube said. "Ten days at most. See you then, Hanson."

Chapter 16

SHOES OF READINESS

Seated in his wicker chair in the cave, Nyx struggled to focus on Rube's book spread open on the table before him. He sighed. At least it was peaceful here. Unlike down in the Temple. It wasn't that he didn't like having his young acolytes around. It was just … well, after living his entire life practically by himself, he really wasn't used to such carrying-on. He wasn't worried so much about the bickering. Silly nonsense that was. It was more the general *noise*. Everything seemed to require shouting and laughter—even things that could be done perfectly well in quiet. Like eating, or getting ready for bed. He shook his head. Undoubtedly there were some romantic tensions playing out, too. Up here, though, he could escape from it all for a while. And concentrate.

It had been five days since he'd brought the book back to Tyrelia. Each day he'd managed to find some time to study it. Interesting reading it made, too. He turned the page. He peered closer. *What was this?* A section on the connections between the Golden City and Tyrelia. *How curious.* He bent over the book. *By the Ancient. Was that a—?*

A cough interrupted him. He looked up in surprise.

Freya materialised. "Excuse me, Brother Nyx. I didn't realise you were up here."

Nyx smiled. "I see your invisibility is coming along nicely," he remarked.

Freya nodded. "Yeah, it's getting easier to sustain it. I made it all the way up the path, completely invisible." She hooked her thumbs in her belt.

Nyx cocked his head. "Are you hiding from someone?"

Freya blushed. "No, not really. Just wanting to be alone for a bit."

"I know that feeling. That's why I came up here myself."

Freya fiddled with her belt. "I'm sorry to have disturbed you. I'll leave you to it." As she turned to go, the mural caught her eye and she stopped. "Brother Nyx, you've been painting again. Is that what you came up here to do?"

Nyx eyed the painting. Now the image portrayed seven figures lined up before an eighth figure, who was bent over, leaning on a staff. He levered himself out of his chair to stand beside her. "No, my child. It's not me painting that."

"What?" Freya turned to stare at him. "But you said you were."

Nyx chuckled. "Actually, my recollection is that Willow asked if I were a painter, and I said 'of sorts'. That's not admitting to painting this mural."

Freya put her hands on her hips. "Who is then? Every time we've come up here, it's been different."

The hermit placed a hand on her shoulder. "This is the Ancient's handiwork," he said simply.

Freya's mouth dropped open. "The Ancient? But why?"

"It's part of the confirmation that you are the One. That Willow and the others are supposed to be here. That you're not alone in this task, Freya."

Freya pushed out a breath. "Sometimes it feels like I am. I've been having these dreams …" Her voice trailed off.

"Hmm?"

Freya rubbed her palms on her tunic as she paced about the cave. "I'm wearing the Armour of Tyrelia and I'm at the head of a massive army, spread out before the Golden City. But then this single arrow comes straight for me and … well, then I wake up. But I think I die." She whispered the last words. Tears welled in her eyes. "I don't know how to fight, Nyx. How am I ever going to be ready to face the Master in battle?"

Nyx shook his head. "Fight? Battle?" he beckoned Freya. "Come, my child, have a seat." Nyx eased himself back into his chair. It creaked as he did so.

She perched opposite him, the book lying open on the table between them.

"It is true that there will be a battle—of sorts. But it won't be fought by a gathering of armies." He wagged a finger. "No. Rather, it will be fought by stealth. For this is not a fight for land or wealth but for truth."

Freya's good eye was huge. "I don't understand. Why am I earning the Armour of Tyrelia, then?"

"My child. The pieces of Armour represent your readiness for this battle of stealth. They are symbols of the lessons you have learned that will protect your heart and mind. That your character has passed the tests life sets for you. But beware, for the Master will try to make you doubt yourself. He is the Master of Lies and will twist and conceal the truth. Why, he even hid the whole of Tyrelia from the inhabitants of Medar."

Freya gripped the arms of her chair. "So, how do we fight this *battle of stealth*?"

Nyx's eyes twinkled. "By telling people the truth, of course."

"But what if we tell them, and they still don't believe?" Freya asked.

Nyx sighed, his mouth downturned. "That could happen, unfortunately. We can't force people to believe in the Ancient or Tyrelia. That's their choice. Our job is simply to tell them."

Freya nodded slowly. "That may be alright for most people in Medar. But what about the people in the Golden City? Even if they believe, they're still trapped by the injection."

"Indeed. That is why we need to determine how to get the Helix River water to them. Talking of which—" Nyx shot a look towards the cave entrance. The sun was setting behind the hills opposite and golden rays illuminated the mural. "—I wonder if Rube or Thyst have had any success yet?" He fished out his talking stone and concentrated on it. The black swirling shapes took on Rube's features. "Brother Rube. You made it out of the City then. What news?"

"Brother Nyx. We have good news. We know the dosage for the antidote."

"What is it?"

"One pouch of water diluted into the drinking water for each level of the City."

"How, by the Ancient, did you figure that out?" Nyx asked.

Rube smiled wryly. "Quite by accident, actually. But there's more. We've managed to get Freya's parents out of the City."

"Where are they?" Freya asked.

Nyx relayed her question to Rube.

"They're here with Thyst and me, hidden not far outside the City. It was quite an adventure getting them out, but that's a story for another time. I'm thinking we should meet up at that obelisk in the Shady Desert. We can deliver Thomas and Martha into your safekeeping, and you can bring us six more pouches of water. Do you agree?"

Nyx nodded. "I'll do more than bring six pouches of water. I'll bring seven new Adelphi with me to help distribute them."

"What?" Rube asked. "That's welcome news. In that case, we'll see you in about five days' time." His face disappeared from the black swirls.

"Do you really think we're ready?" Freya asked.

Nyx leaned forward on his staff. "The question is, do *you* think you're ready?"

Freya went very still and studied her hands. Then she lifted her chin. "Yes, Brother Nyx. Yes, I do. Oh," she gasped, looking down at her feet.

Nyx's knuckles whitened. "Is it …?"

Freya beamed at him. She lifted a foot. Sunlight glinted off the material encasing it. Metal. "Yep. I just got the shoes. I guess I really am ready."

Chapter 17

BARRICADE

Their horses were where they'd left them. But now there were four people, and only two horses. Rube chewed his lip. "Thyst's horse can carry both her and Martha, but my old Cirrus can't carry both Thomas and me."

"We'll have to take turns with one or two of us walking, then," Thyst suggested.

"Or …" Rube said.

"Or what?" Thyst asked.

Rube pressed his mouth into a line. "Or I stay here."

"What?" said Thyst. "No, you can't."

Rube inclined his chin. He had already decided. "There's something I need to do," he said.

"Which would be?" Thomas asked.

Rube shrugged. "I should hang around. Keep my finger on the mood of the City. Besides, with this leg I'll just slow you all down."

Thyst's expression softened. She placed a hand on his arm. "Alright then, Rube. Be careful."

"You too," he said. He turned himself invisible and left them standing in the copse of trees.

~

Getting back into the City was going to be a lot more challenging than he'd anticipated. Activity had ramped up around the gate, which meant more chance of bumping into someone. He crept closer to get a better look. Guards traipsed back and forth, carrying sacks of something on their shoulders into the City from a cart parked this side of the drawbridge. The fields were empty. The farmers still weren't permitted outside the City, then. What were the Guards doing? Moving flour? Grain? Whatever the contents of the sacks, they appeared to be heavy. He crept closer to the cart and prodded one of the sacks. It gave a little, but not much, and made a slight squeaking sound. It felt like … yes, sand. *Interesting.*

He trailed one of the Guards, not too close so as to be sensed, but close enough to give him unimpeded passage in the man's wake. *By the Land!* The Guards were sandbagging up the entranceways. *No time to waste.* He scurried back over the drawbridge to the copse of trees. The others had long gone.

He whipped out his stone. "Brother Nyx," he plunged in. "The Guards are barricading the entrance to the Golden City. What are we going to do?"

Nyx tutted. "Then we'll just have to find another way in."

Rube threw a hand in the air in frustration, raking his knuckles on a tree. "Ouch. There *is* no other way, Brother Nyx. I've tried." He sucked his knuckle.

Nyx hummed. "Perhaps you haven't tried *everything.*"

"What do you mean?"

"I've been reading that book you gave me on Tyrelia. It has some interesting information in it. Things we Adelphi had no knowledge of," Nyx said.

"Like what? A secret passageway?" Rube asked eagerly.

"Of sorts, yes," Nyx replied enigmatically.

"Where is it?"

"I'll tell you when you get to the obelisk," Nyx said.

"I'm not going to the obelisk. I've decided to stick around the Golden City," Rube replied.

"In that case, I'll meet you there. How long will it take you to get to Level Seven?" Nyx asked.

"Level Seven?" Rube was taken aback. "Three days, all going well. Four tops."

Nyx nodded. "And how long before Thyst arrives at the obelisk?"

"All going to plan, they should arrive in three days' time."

"Good. See you at the well in Level Seven in three days from today. Tuesday."

Rube jerked his chin. "Tuesday. Unless …"

"Unless what?"

Rube puckered his lips. "What if the Master has blocked up this other secret passageway too?"

Nyx chuckled. "You mean like he put the Wall up to block people from leaving Medar? No, Rube. The Master can't stop us. You'll see."

"I hope you're right, Brother Nyx. I really do."

"Have faith, Brother Rube. Remember, the Master is only as powerful as you believe him to be."

"If you say so," Rube said. "I'd better go now, otherwise I might not make it back into the Golden City. Goodbye, Brother Nyx. See you Tuesday." He closed his fist, extinguishing the red glow, and set off for the City. By the Ancient, he hoped Brother Nyx was right. These had better not be his last moments outside the Golden City. There was still too much to be done. Gritting his teeth, he limped over the drawbridge, wove his way between Guards carrying sandbags, and slipped through the last unblocked archway. *Made it. That was close.*

Chapter 18

THE OBELISK

"Can you see anything yet?" Freya asked for the tenth time. She jiggled from leg to leg.

Willow scanned the deepening darkness. "Nope, nothing."

Brother Nyx appeared from behind the obelisk. "Thyst just contacted me. Who wants to flash the signal?"

"Can I?" Freya asked.

"Are you sure you won't drop your stone?" Willow teased.

Freya pulled a face. "I'm just excited, is all." Balancing her stone on her palm, she focussed on Thyst. A bright white glow formed a halo around the stone. She covered the light with her free hand three times in quick succession, causing bursts of light to pierce the darkness, then cut the connection.

"There," Willow said, pointing. Off to their left, three purple flashes answered their signal.

Two large lumpy shapes emerged from the darkness: two horses carrying riders.

"Ma! Da!" Freya called.

The human shapes slid off the horses and ran towards her.

Freya ran too. She flung herself into her mother's embrace. Her father wrapped his arms around them both. They cried and laughed at the same time.

"It's so good to see you again," Freya said.

Martha squeezed her and stepped back, holding her at arms' length. "You too, Freya. You've changed, though. And what are you wearing?"

Freya's cheeks grew hot. "This? It's the Armour of Tyrelia," she said.

Nyx shuffled forward. "This is a wonderful family reunion, but it grows dark. Come, let's go inside the obelisk where it's more comfortable. Thyst, there's a ring to lash the horses to, set into the tower over there."

Thyst led the horses away, while Freya wrapped her arms around her parents and practically skipped between them. "I've got so many people to introduce you to," she said. "First of all, there's Brother Nyx, whom you have just met. He's the leader of the Adelphi. This is Willow—my best friend."

Willow doffed an imaginary hat.

"Nice to meet you," Thomas said.

Martha let go of Freya and held her arms open to Willow. "Thank you, Willow, for looking out for our Freya. We've heard some of your adventures." She hugged her.

Willow grinned. "That's a better welcome than my parents gave Freya. Thank you."

They rounded the obelisk to be greeted by a large entranceway. Light spilled from within down a short flight of stairs at their feet. Freya tugged her parents inside. The chamber was crammed with people.

"Oh my," Martha said. "There's more."

"Of course. These are the new Adelphi, Ma and Da. Let me introduce you to Alex—he's Willow's twin—" Unexpectedly, her voice squeaked. She felt her ma's eyes on her, and her face grew hot again. "—Peri, Turq, Amber, and Di," she rushed, pointing in turn. "Everyone, these are my parents, Thomas and Martha. And Watcher Thyst."

The Adelphi murmured greetings to the newcomers.

Nyx hobbled into the obelisk and tapped his staff lightly on the ground. "We'll spend the night here. We make our move at first light."

"Why wait?" Willow asked. "Why not go now? Surely the cover of darkness would give us the element of surprise."

"I think we'll achieve the element of surprise when we go at dawn. And I don't think it's a good idea for you all to be stumbling around an unfamiliar city in the dark."

"Fair enough," Willow said.

"What about Ma and Da?" Freya asked. "Are you going to warp them back to Tyrelia now?"

"No. Until we are sure that they can't see the Wall, it's too risky warping them into Tyrelia."

He didn't say it, but Freya understood. Warping unbelievers through the Wall would kill them. "So, if you're not going to warp them, how will they get to Tyrelia from here?"

Nyx laid his hand on her shoulder. "I will guide them back myself."

Freya gawped at him. "What? I thought you were going to take us to the secret passage into the Golden City?"

Nyx chuckled. "I am, my child. I will get you there, but then I will come straight back here for your parents. Someone needs to guide them, and I'm afraid I'm not nimble enough to be of much use inside the City."

Freya nodded, chewing her lip. "I suppose you're right. Thank you, Brother Nyx." Impulsively, she threw her arms around him.

He stumbled back a few steps and clutched her arm to steady himself. He patted her back. "No need to thank me. I feel it's me who should be thanking *you*, for giving this old man the pleasure of seeing the prophecy unfold before his very eyes." He blinked rapidly. "No, no need to thank me at all."

~

They took turns keeping watch during the night. Now it was Freya's turn. She should have been tired, what with staying up late, talking to her ma and da, catching up on everything they'd been up to since being separated all those months ago. But she wasn't. She was excited.

As the sky transitioned through a deep purple to the light grey of early dawn, Freya roused the others. It was time.

With a subdued air, they tidied up their belongings and checked the waterskins. They each carried two: one to use, and a spare one in case something happened to the first. Or—and nobody had verbalised this—in case something happened to one of them. Freya hugged her parents tightly. She'd only just found them and now she was leaving them again. Too soon. "I'll see you in Tyrelia, and I'll bring Jack, too," she promised.

Thyst was petting the horses. "What shall we do with them, Brother Nyx?" she asked.

"I've been thinking about that," he said. Bending his head close to hers, he muttered, "I think you'd best let them go. They'll find their way back to some town or other. Better they maybe get a little hungry than definitely get eaten if we leave them here."

"Eaten?" Thomas asked, stepping outside, his arm around Freya. "What would eat them?"

Nyx jumped. "Oh. Heh. You startled me."

Thomas looked from Nyx to Thyst. "Well?" he asked.

"Gnomes live in the tunnel which leads from this obelisk to Yawbridge, Da," Freya explained.

"But you'll be fine if you stay nice and close to this entrance.

I'll only be gone for a few minutes," Nyx added.

"Oh," Thomas said. He lifted an eyebrow at Freya. "I don't think I need worry your mother unnecessarily with this piece of information."

Freya shook her head quickly. "She'll just get herself worked up. Like Brother Nyx said, he'll be back before you know it."

"Talking of which, it's time to go," Nyx announced.

Freya squeezed her da then her ma, who'd come to stand on the steps beside her husband. Freya joined Brother Nyx and the others. They all linked arms. Freya smiled at her parents. "See you in Tyrelia," she called. Humming filled the air. Her parents blurred, then disappeared in a rush of colours, to be replaced seconds later by an empty, still plaza. It was early morning and deathly quiet.

They stood grouped beside an unfamiliar pillar. "Where are we?" Freya whispered.

"This, my young acolytes, is Level Seven of the Golden City," Nyx replied.

"There's a Law Pillar in the Golden City?" Willow asked.

"Hush. Yes. Now, quickly, go to the well. There it is. Behind us."

"Brother Nyx? Is that you?" A voice floated on the air. Rube materialised briefly next to the well.

Freya ran to him, allowing herself likewise to become visible. "Rube! Father," she whispered. She threw herself into his arms.

"Well met," Brother Nyx said in a low voice. He, too, embraced Rube, then shuffled to the well and tipped in his skin of water. "That's me done." He beamed at them. "Good luck, everyone, and see you back in Tyrelia."

Chapter 19

A SANDSTORM

Thomas blinked. "They're gone," he stated. He'd seen Rube and, more recently, Thyst make themselves invisible, but this was something else.

"To think, our daughter an Adelphi," Martha murmured.

"How did they do that?" Thomas asked.

"And did you see that armour?" Martha continued.

Suddenly, a shape materialised in front of them.

"Brother Nyx, you're back," Thomas said. "How did it go?"

Nyx leaned heavily on his staff. "Good. They're safely inside the City and have met up with Rube. Now freedom for the inhabitants of the Golden City rests in their hands. Your freedom, on the other hand, rests in mine." He chuckled.

A wind slithered along the ground and lifted Nyx's robes. Nyx scrutinised the sky. "We'd better get moving," he said.

He set off due north. They hadn't got far before the wind got stronger. It swirled around them, picking up grains of sand and flicking them into their clothing, hair, eyes and mouths. Nyx squinted towards the horizon. A dark cloud was gathering. "This is no good. Let's go back to the obelisk. There's another way. Underground."

"That sounds much better," Martha said.

Nyx grunted. "Perhaps," he said.

The wind grew stronger still, whipping their clothing about them. Thomas shielded his face with his arm and picked up his pace. The bulk of the obelisk loomed. He guided Martha into the entrance. Nyx stumbled in behind them. They stamped and shook out their clothing. Little piles of sand formed around their feet.

Martha ran her fingers through her hair. "Ugh, it's all gritty."

Nyx faced them. "I've never travelled this tunnel. I saw it marked on a map in the book about Tyrelia that Rube gave me. It may not exist any longer."

"Well, there's only one way to find out, isn't there?" Martha said.

Nyx's gaze flicked to Thomas, then returned to Martha. "There's more. There's another tunnel and ..." He fidgeted with his staff.

"And what?" Martha put her hands on her hips. "Spit it out." She glanced at Thomas. At the look on Thomas's face, her eyes narrowed. "What aren't you telling me?" she demanded.

Nyx sighed. "The other tunnel—the one that runs towards Yawbridge—is infested with gnomes," he stated. "We don't know whether they're in this other one, too."

Martha looked from one to the other. "Gnomes," she said. "You think I'm scared of a few gnomes, after what we've been through in the Golden City?"

Thomas hung his head, his voice barely audible. "You might have been."

Martha tsked. "Thomas Farmer," she reprimanded. "I've managed quite a few things, lately, while you were hiding in that printing press. Including dealing with Guards. So, I think

I'll be okay with a few gnomes."

"Well, there might be more than just a few," Nyx pointed out.

Martha lifted her chin. "As I said, there's only one way to find out."

Nyx chuckled. "Should've realised where Freya gets her pluck from. Follow me."

He fumbled in his robes and withdrew his talking stone. In three paces, he stood at the top of the flight of stairs, which stretched down and down into utter blackness. He illuminated his stone and began the descent. Martha followed him, and Thomas brought up the rear.

As they went down, the air grew warmer. It smelled like earth, overlain with another, slightly unpleasant odour. When they reached the bottom, Nyx stopped and turned slowly, holding out his stone. There were two tunnels. "Looks like the tunnel is still intact," he said quietly. He waved a hand towards one. "That's the one." As they moved towards it, a rhythmic, slapping sound reached their ears. Nyx immediately extinguished his stone. He shoved Martha and Thomas into the second tunnel, crowding in behind them. "Keep moving down the tunnel," he whispered.

They crept forwards, brushing their fingertips against the rough wall. The slapping followed them. Then stopped. Thomas breathed a sigh of relief. But then he tripped and went down heavily on to one knee. He cried out as pain sliced through his leg. He rolled on the ground, clutching his knee.

"Hush, man," Nyx hissed.

Thomas squeezed his eyes shut and clenched his teeth. Despite the agony, he heard it. The slapping. The slaps grew louder and increased in frequency. Grunting, he scrabbled back against the wall, with his leg at an awkward angle.

Martha crouched beside him and placed her arm around his shoulders. "Are you hurt badly?" she asked.

"I'm not sure," Thomas replied. He strained to see what was happening. Suddenly, a flash of light illuminated the tunnel. The image seared onto his retinas: Nyx, facing down two squat, pot-bellied figures with large, flappy ears. The two gnomes, startled by the sudden brightness, flung their arms over their eyes. Nyx whacked his staff onto the skull of first one, then the other, and they dropped like felled trees.

Nyx turned to Thomas and Martha. "Can you walk, Thomas?" he asked.

"Let me try." Thomas pushed himself upright. He tested his weight on the leg. A stab of pain shot through him and he grunted. "I can if I can lean on someone," he said.

"Let's go then," Nyx said.

A blood curdling howl filled the air, and a small figure launched itself at Nyx, grabbing him around the neck.

Thomas yelled.

Nyx stumbled backwards, snatching at the arms wrapped around his throat. He dropped his stone. Instantly, darkness engulfed them. There were grunts and scuffling, then all went quiet.

"Brother Nyx?" Thomas asked uncertainly.

"I'm all right."

There was a scraping noise, then Nyx's stone glowed. Nyx knelt, panting on the ground, the gnome dead beside him. He rolled the gnome off his staff and levered himself to his feet with the aid of his stick.

"Let's get out of here, before any more turn up," Thomas said.

Slap, slap, slap.

"Too late," Nyx said. He thrust his stone into Martha's

hands. "Here, take this. Keep it safe. Follow the tunnel. It will lead you to a stairway down into the Chasm then a bridge across it. As long as you believe in the Ancient, you will be able to pass through the Wall and into Tyrelia. Now go!"

"But—" Martha protested.

"Go!" Nyx roared. He disappeared into the gloom.

Thomas draped his arm around Martha's shoulders, leaning on her for support. As they hobbled forwards, the ground trembled and small rocks dislodged from above, bouncing off their shoulders.

Martha stumbled. "What's happening?" she asked.

Thomas craned his neck to peer behind them. The ground tilted underfoot. A rumbling filled the air as rocks tumbled to the ground. He coughed on dust. "It's a rockfall—"

Then everything went black.

Chapter 20

WATERSKINS

In the grey dawn, the Adelphi gathered around Rube at the Level Seven well. "Do you all know which level you're going to?" Rube asked in a hoarse whisper.

They nodded.

"Here. Take some of these pamphlets and scatter them around the level once you've dosed the well."

Freya held one up to her good eye. "*Drink the water to be free from the Master's tyranny,*" she read. A symbol took up the bottom half of the pamphlet. Like a number eight lying on its side, one portion of it disintegrating into dots. She peered more closely at it. No, not dots. Little birds flapping away. "Nice," she said. "What's with the number eight?"

"That was Hanson's idea," Rube said. "It's a symbol for 'infinity'. Together with the birds, it means *infinitely free*. A nice touch, don't you think? Now, the wells are roughly in the same location on each level: to the left of the bottom gate, as you head downhill. So, for Level Six, for example, you'd need to go almost to the gate for Level Five, then veer left before going through. Understand?"

"Yes," Amber said. "Let's go."

"Wait," Rube said. "Each level has its own … how can I put it, *mood*. Don't let it affect you."

"What do you mean by *mood*?" Turq asked.

"Level Six is called *Gula*—who's going there?"

Amber and Di raised their hands.

"*Gula* means 'gluttony': everyone there is fat and eats constantly."

"Doesn't sound too dangerous," Amber giggled.

"Who's going to Level Five?" Rube asked.

Peri and Turq raised their hands.

"That might pose more of a risk. Level Five—*Luxuria*—seems to be all about lust. Watch out for temptation," Rube warned.

Turq smirked. "Sounds like fun," he said.

"On second thoughts, I want you two to swap with the girls. Safer that way," Rube said.

"But—" Turq protested.

"No buts," Rube cut him off. "Now, who's going to Level Four?"

"That will be us," Willow said, jerking her thumb at Alex.

"Do you have anger issues?" Rube asked.

"What? No," Alex said.

"That level is called *Ira* and it makes everyone angry."

"They should be fine there," Freya chipped in. "On the other hand, if there's a level with a mood of mischief, then you should avoid sending them there at all costs."

Rube blinked. "No, there's no mischief level. Thyst, that leaves you to deal with Level Three. That's *Avaritia*—greed."

Thyst nodded.

"And Freya, I'll accompany you to Level Two. It's called *Superbia* and has a mood of pride over it. Also, I can show you where Jack lives."

"Great. Thanks, Rube."

"Now, remember, in and out. Don't let yourselves be seen. Particularly avoid the Master. See you back in Tyrelia."

They all turned themselves invisible, and set off in pairs, apart from Thyst, who joined Rube and Freya, seeing as their route was identical for four levels.

"You know," Freya ventured after a while, "it's so great being able to turn myself invisible. Not having to rely on someone else to do it for me."

Thyst agreed. "Remember fleeing for our lives from Yawbridge, constantly pursued by Guards, up and over the Andoria mountains?"

Freya pulled a face. "How could I forget. And the whole time, I had it in me to make myself invisible."

"Because you had Tyrelian blood," Rube agreed. "Except you didn't know it."

"No." Freya sighed. "But I know it now. I'm glad I found you, Father."

Rube patted her shoulder. "Me too, Freya. But now we need to be quiet. The City is waking."

They continued in silence, heading ever downhill, sticking to the edge of the road and avoiding people. It was late afternoon by the time they farewelled Thyst in Level Three. The tenth bell had already tolled. "Why is it getting so busy?" Freya whispered.

"The working day is over. Everyone's heading home now," Rube explained. "The well is this way." He grabbed her arm and guided her towards the well.

When they got there, people were queued up waiting to draw water.

"Bother," Rube hissed. "We have to hurry." He prodded Freya forwards.

Freya's heart hammered. This was it. This was the moment she'd been training for. She untied the string attaching the waterskin to her belt. But as she pulled it loose, it slipped from her fingers and dropped to the ground. *Splat.* The skin burst open as it landed. "Oh no," Freya yelped, then clapped her hand to her mouth. *It's okay. That's why I brought a second skin.*

A woman screamed at the sudden appearance of the burst waterskin at her feet, and stumbled backwards, knocking over the person behind her.

Freya took advantage of the confusion to complete her task. She grabbed her second pouch of water, untied it, and quickly tipped it into the well. It was done. She raced back to Rube.

"Shall we distribute our pamphlets now?" she whispered.

"I think we should wait until there's fewer people." He pressed Freya against the wall.

She leaned her head back, then eased to a sitting position, careful not to scrape her shield. Apart from a half-hour rest in Level Five to eat their lunch, they'd been walking all day. Her stomach growled, and she pressed her hand into it, trying to suppress the rumbling.

Before long, the queues dissipated. "Alright, let's do it," Rube whispered.

"Are you sure?" she asked. "There are still some people around."

"It will add to the mystery," Rube assured her. "Go for it."

Freya flung her hand out, releasing the pamphlets. They instantly materialised and fluttered gently to the ground, like autumn leaves freed from a branch by a sudden gust of wind. The same thing happened from where Rube was standing.

Freya dashed out of the plaza to exclamations of wonder. She ran to the first door down the alley, as agreed, and waited, panting, her hands on her knees. Shortly, Rube joined her.

"That was fun," Freya whispered.

"Wasn't it?" Rube agreed. "And now, let's go find Hank and Leena," Rube whispered.

"Don't you mean Jack?" Freya asked.

"Yes, but first I'd like to speak to Hank and Leena, and young Sam. We'll need to spend the night somewhere, and I'm sure they'll take us in."

"Who are they?" Freya asked.

Rube paused. "Of course. You don't know. They are very, very close friends of your parents. We can trust them completely. This way." He led her back uphill, a right here and a left there, to a white-washed cottage with pots of red geraniums sitting on the window-sills. "Around the back," Rube instructed.

They skirted the building.

"Wait here," Rube said, placing a hand on her shoulder.

She waited at the base of a short flight of stairs at the rear of the house. Rube's footsteps echoed as he climbed, followed by three short, sharp knocks on the door, a gap, and three more. Quick footsteps sounded from inside the house, then the door was flung open. A man peered out. His head was covered in a mop of brown curls, and he sported a full beard. "Rube?" he asked in a hoarse whisper.

"Yes, it's me," Rube replied. "And I've got Freya with me."

Freya ran lightly up the stairs and inside. The door closed of its own accord behind her.

"Leena," the man called. "Come quickly."

"What is it?" a woman's voice replied from the hallway.

"You'll never believe who's here," the man said.

Rube allowed himself to become visible, and Freya followed suit. They stood side-by-side as the woman entered the kitchen. She stopped short, taking in Freya's strange attire. Then she flew to Rube and hugged him. "Rube, you came back. You found us. How?"

"As I passed through two days ago, I scouted around. I guessed that the printing press would be in the same location as the warehouse in Level One. I followed Hank home," he admitted.

Leena tutted. "And who is this? Is it Freya?"

Rube chuckled. "Yes, Leena. This is my—and Martha and Thomas's—daughter, Freya. She is the One." He laid his arm around her shoulders and squeezed gently.

"Well, my dear, it is an absolute privilege to meet you," Leena said, hugging her.

"And I'm Hank," the man said. He stepped towards her, his hand outstretched.

Freya shook it awkwardly. "It's a pleasure to meet you both," she said. She took a deep breath. "Do you happen to know where my brother, Jack, is?"

A strange expression crossed Leena's features. She shot a look at her husband, then said, "Yes, we do, Freya. He's sharing a house with two young men. I take it you'd like to talk to him?"

"Yes."

"Tell you what. How about we have dinner first? I'll send Sam to ask Jack to pop around afterwards."

"Good idea, Leena," Rube said, sinking into a chair with a groan. "I'm sorry, but we've been on our feet all day, and these old bones are mighty weary."

Freya shrugged off her shield and rested it against a wall. "Is it okay to put this here?" she asked.

A young boy entered the room. "What's all the talking ..." his eyes landed on the shield. "Whoa. What's *that*? Who are you?" he asked Freya.

Freya pulled off her helmet and tucked it under her arm. "Sam, is it? I'm Freya. Martha and—"

"I know," Sam said, excitement in his voice. "You're Jack's sister. You're *the One!* Did you really knock down the Wall? And are you gonna kill the Master?" he asked, his cheeks flushed.

"Hush, Sam, keep your voice down, son," Hank growled. "You'll bring the Master to our doorstep with your carrying on." He clipped him playfully around the ear.

"Sorry Da," Sam said.

Freya smiled at Sam. She was getting used to people thinking she was special, but she wasn't going to let it go to her head. Not this time. There was too much at stake. "I guess I am the One. But no, I didn't knock down the Wall. And no, I'm not going to kill the Master," she said gently. *I hope. Unless he tries to kill me.*

Sam's face fell. "What *did* you do, then?" he asked. "And how come you've got all that cool armour?"

Freya fingered her belt. "I found the long-lost path to Tyrelia. And I figured out how to pass *through* the Wall. And, now that I've earned the Armour of Tyrelia, along with the other Adelphi, we're going to free everyone from the Golden City. And Medar."

Sam's mouth formed an 'o'.

Leena pressed her hand to her mouth. "Well, in that case, I imagine you'll need a good meal in your belly. Sam, run over to Jack's and ask him to pop around after dinner, will you? Do *not* mention Freya." She grabbed his shoulders and stooped to catch his eye. Nodding briefly, she released him with a squeeze. "In about two hours' time should be fine."

"Sure thing, Ma." Sam raced out the front door, slamming it behind him.

Leena leaned against the bench. "Well then," she said, "that's quite a lot to take in." She thought for a moment. "It's good to see you again, Rube," she said, "Tell me, how are Martha and Thomas?"

Rube ran a hand through his hair. "They've left the Golden City. The whole of Level One has been freed."

"Freed?" Hank asked. "But how?"

Rube laced his fingers. "We accidentally dropped a pouch of Helix water into the Level One well. Then, the next day, there was an incident with an ox outside the City. The farmers scattered. They should've died … but they didn't. Well, some did. But most didn't. That's when we realised that the power of the injection had been broken."

"I thought there was an infectious outbreak in Level One. I had to print some posters about it," Hank said.

Rube nodded. "I know, but that's a lie. The Master doesn't want anyone to know. Quite a few inhabitants from Level One escaped. But now the main gate has been barricaded. I got Martha and Thomas out just in time."

Leena tilted her head, thinking. "Freya, you said that you're going to free *everyone* from the Golden City?" She looked up, her eyes full of hope.

"That's right. The other Adelphi and I have put doses of Helix water into the wells of each level of the City today. Then we distributed these pamphlets." She extracted one from her tunic and held it out.

Hank snatched it from her hand. He scanned it quickly, then whistled. "Nice work. Where did you get these done?" he asked.

Rube smiled. "From your successor, actually. His name is Hanson. Nice man. We met him while getting Thomas out."

Hank scratched his beard. "Figures," he said. He handed the

pamphlet to Leena.

Her eyes widened as she read it. "But … if the Master has barricaded the front gate, even if we've drunk the water, how do we get out?"

Freya grinned at Rube. "Same way we got in. We warp."

Chapter 21

JACK'S CHOICE

There was a knock on the door. They ceased talking.

"That'll be Jack," Leena said. Her chair scraped as she stood to answer the door. "Come on in, Jack," she said. "There are some people here to see you."

"Who?" Jack asked. Then he stopped in his tracks. "Freya?" Leena closed the door behind him.

Freya leapt from her chair and threw herself at her brother. Unbidden, tears sprang from her eyes. "Jack! It's so good to see you again."

"Freya, you too. How did you get here?" he demanded, holding her at arms' length.

"It's a long story," she said. "You'd better sit down."

"Let's all go through to the lounge, shall we?" Leena suggested. "I'll get some tea."

Once they were settled, Jack looked at Freya expectantly.

"I'm not quite sure where to start," Freya said.

"Maybe why you're here in the Golden City?" Jack said. "Ma and Da spent the whole time trying to figure out how to get out to find you, and now you turn up here." He looked at her quizzically. "Talking of which, why are you *here*, in Level

Two? Why aren't you in Level One with Ma and Da?"

"They aren't in Level One, Jack. They've left the Golden City and are on their way to Tyrelia. They might already be in Tyrelia now, as we speak," Rube said.

Jack snorted. "Tyrelia. Are you serious?"

Freya caught his hand. "Yes, I am. It's real, Jack, and it's *amazing*. It's beautiful, and there's plenty of food for everyone—the Ancient provides. He's a good ruler. He really cares for you. All you have to do is obey his Laws. And Tyrelia's so much brighter than here. Did you know the whole of Medar is covered in cloud? Everything is so *grey* here. Dull. And look at my skin." She let go of his hand and pulled back her sleeve to expose her forearm. Light played under the skin, making her skin appear translucent.

Jack studied her arm. "That's … nice. But what's that got to do with me?" he asked.

Freya was taken aback. "I've come to free you from the Golden City. Well, not just you. Everybody. And take you back to Tyrelia. You do want to come, don't you?"

Jack looked down at his hands. "I dunno. The Golden City's not so bad. I'm doing okay here."

"Not so bad?" Freya asked. "But you've been trapped here and oppressed. Now you can leave." She threw her hands wide.

"Did you say something about obeying laws in Tyrelia?" Jack asked.

"Yes, of course," Freya said. "But they're good laws. Easy to follow. Like *'Honour the Ancient'*, *'Put others first'*, *'Use your gifts for good'* and *'Follow the Rules'*."

"Hmph. As I thought," Jack mumbled. "Laws, rules. Sounds like hard work to me."

Freya balled her fists. "They're not hard work at all. Why,

the first Rule I came across was to *quench my thirst*," she protested.

"Still," Jack said. "Maybe it's easy for someone like you to follow them. Not someone like me, though."

"What do you mean 'someone like you'?" Freya asked. "We're the same."

Jack hung his head. "No, we're not," he mumbled. "I'm a bad person. I've made mistakes."

Freya's mouth dropped open. Then she snapped it shut. "You think I haven't made mistakes?" she asked. "Let me tell you, I've made some *really* bad mistakes. But you know what? Our mistakes don't define us. It's the choices we make going forward that define us. *Better* choices. That's one lesson I've learned the hard way."

Jack turned away. "No, it's too late for me," he said.

Freya put a hand on his shoulder. "Don't be silly, Jack. It's not too late. It's *never* too late."

Jack shrugged her hand off. "It is for me, Freya. I'm staying here. I like the Golden City. Besides, I don't want to serve some Ancient. I like ruling my own life."

"Jack," Rube tried. "You may think that you're ruling your own life, but if you choose to *not* serve the Ancient, then you're choosing to serve the Master."

Abruptly, Jack stood up. "What's wrong with serving the Master? I've got a good enough life here. Goodbye, Freya. Rube. Everyone." He strode out of the room and down the hallway. The front door slammed.

Freya jumped up, tears streaming down her cheeks. "Jack."

Rube laid a hand on her arm, restraining her. "Leave him, Freya. He's made his choice."

"But I want him to come to Tyrelia," Freya said. "I promised Ma and Da." She slumped onto the sofa.

"I know," Rube agreed. "But that's the problem with freedom. Yes, people are free to leave. But they're also free to stay. We can't force anyone, Freya. You tried, and that's all that can be expected."

Freya sighed. "Oh Father, what am I going to do now?"

Rube smiled gently. "The only thing we can do. Keep trying."

Chapter 22

EXODUS

It began before the first bell. Rube had gone down into Level One at first light, to get Hanson and to distribute the pamphlets. But he'd come back with more than just Hanson and his family: the group was about forty strong. And now they were all clustered around outside Hank and Leena's house. Rube had given up trying to keep them invisible, so now the neighbours had emerged and were asking what the commotion was.

Hank flung open the front door. Hank, Leena and Sam sidled out and stood off to the side. Then Freya stepped onto the porch, resplendent in her Armour. A gasp went up. "People of the Golden City," she said. "If you have drunk water from the well, then the power of the injection is broken, and you are free to leave."

"How is this possible?" somebody called.

"I, and my fellow Adelphi," Freya beckoned Rube to come and stand beside her, "have infused the wells with water from the River Helix in Tyrelia."

"Tyrelia? Where's that?"

"Do you know the prophecy about the Girl breaking down

155

the Wall?" Rube asked.

A murmur went through the crowd, and many nodded their heads. "This is that Girl!" Rube announced.

"The Master has been lying to us," Freya continued. "He led us to believe that Medar is all there is. That there is nothing beyond the Wall. But there *is* something beyond the Wall, and it's called Tyrelia. I know, because I've been there."

Exclamations of surprise rippled through the gathering. The volume rose.

Freya held up a hand for silence. "Tyrelia is a wonderful place, and it's governed by a benevolent ruler called the Ancient. It's his tears that form the Helix River. It's his tears that have freed you from the injection." She paused to allow the people to process this, then held her hand up once more. "If you choose to believe in the Ancient, then follow me, and I will take you to Tyrelia."

Somebody whooped. The noise took on a tone of excitement. "Come on, then," a man called. "What are we waiting for? Let's go."

Rube nudged Freya.

She held her sword aloft. "Up to Level Seven. Follow me," she declared. She leapt off the steps and headed up the street.

"Shouldn't we be going down into Level One?" someone asked.

"No," replied someone else, "we're from there. The Guards have blocked the city gates."

"It's alright," Leena chipped in. "The Adelphi have found another way out."

The crowd followed Freya, babbling excitedly. Within a few moments, they arrived at the gate to Level Three. Freya paused. "If you've drunk the water, you are safe to pass through."

"What did she say?" someone muttered, "I can't see or hear

her."

A young lad darted off.

Freya turned to face the gate. A Guard leaned over from the parapet above them. "You there," he commanded. "Stop, in the name of the Master."

Freya squinted at him. Ugh, his skin was grey, his eyes dull. He looked ... rotten. He had no authority over her. "I don't serve the Master," Freya replied, and she marched through the gate.

The crowd hesitated, then followed in a surge.

"It's okay," someone said.

"I'm through unharmed," exclaimed another.

"The power of the injection is truly broken," said a third.

A commotion broke out. Angry shouts and yells. Then the crowd parted hurriedly to admit a lad leading a beautiful, white stallion.

Freya turned, and the lad bowed awkwardly. He held out the reins to Freya. "Your ... Grace," he said.

Freya took the reins. "I'm no *Grace*," she said, "Just Freya. And thank you." She admired the animal and stroked its neck. He looked exactly like the one in her dreams. "What's his name?"

"Starlight," the lad said.

"Starlight. Perfect." With a single fluid movement, she swung herself up into the saddle. "Onwards," she called and spurred Starlight forwards.

Rube and the group called out to the Level Three inhabitants as they passed. "Come and join us if you've drunk the well water," Rube said.

"You've been freed from the injection," said another.

"We came from Level Two and nothing happened when we went through the gate," claimed another.

The throng swelled as another fifty or sixty people joined the group.

As she trotted through Level Three, Freya's confidence grew. She had done it. She'd led these poor people out of their enslavement. She tossed her head. The snug helmet felt right. Of course it did; it belonged to her. She deserved the Armour of Tyrelia. In fact, she should probably be receiving more praise than she was getting. She looked down her nose at the people trailing behind her. Maybe they should show her some sign of allegiance. Pledge their lives to her, or something.

"Halt! In the name of the Master."

The command jolted her out of her reverie. A line of Guards blocked the gateway to Level Four. Her mount shied, and she struggled to regain control.

At that moment, somebody screamed from the back of the crowd. Shouts echoed, and people jostled and pressed forwards.

"Stop pushing," one man complained.

"You're squashing me," said another.

Freya wheeled her horse. "What's happening?" she demanded.

"Guards!" someone shouted. "They're attacking us from behind."

The crowd surged and heaved, as people pushed this way and that. This wasn't how it was supposed to happen. Now what?

"Freya," Rube called. "What are you doing? Keep going."

She closed her eyes. Remembered Brother Nyx's words. *It's a battle of wills, not of swords.* What was the Master's will? To keep the people trapped in the Golden City. What did the Ancient want? To set them free. Only one thing for it, then.

Freya walked Starlight right up to the wall of Guards. Stared into their slack, grey faces. "No," she said. "I don't serve the Master. *You* move, in the name of the Ancient."

They held their ground.

She yanked on her reins, and Starlight reared, whinnying, his hooves thrashing.

Three Guards dropped to their knees, shields raised, protecting their heads from the menace.

"Charge," Freya yelled, and galloped through the Guards. They scattered, and the people surged in her wake, through the gateway into Level Four.

Once the adrenalin had worn off, she slowed her mount. Those foolish Guards. Thinking they could stop her. How *dare* they. She ground her teeth. If there were any more waiting for her, they'd be sorry. She spurred her horse forward once more.

"Freya, slow down."

She paused, looking around. Oh, that's right. Rube was there. How could she have forgotten? It was just that those Guards blocking her way and attacking them from behind had made her feel so angry. *Angry.*

"Rube, what's the mood over this level?" she asked, leaning down from her saddle.

"That'd be *Ira*—anger," he replied. "Why?"

"That explains it," she said, grimly. "We may be immune to the forces confining people to the levels, but it would seem I'm not immune to the moods. I'm feeling angry. And in the previous level, I felt a bit … never mind."

"What?"

Heat flooded her cheeks, and she tugged at her collar. "Proud," she mumbled, "and greedy."

Rube patted her leg, his eyes worried. "Hang in there, Freya," he said. "Only three more levels to go."

She approached the Level Five gate with apprehension. No

Guards blocked the way. She frowned. Was it a trap? She scanned her surroundings. No one. Cautiously, she walked Starlight through the gateway. Nothing happened. She released her breath. It was alright. She urged her horse forward once more, scanning the buildings. She sniffed. "What's that scent?" she asked.

Rube lifted his nose. "Oh yes. Musk. And see those red curtains?" He waved a hand.

Freya eyed the floaty gauze drifting from a nearby window. Another one, four houses further down.

"They indicate, er …" Rube's face turned a funny colour. "… brothels."

Freya stared at him blankly. "What's a brothel?" she asked.

Rube shoved his hands in his deep pockets. "They're places where … ah … adults … express their love. For payment." His face was now a deep red. He hurried up to her mount's head and grabbed the bridle, inspecting it closely.

Freya studied his glowing scalp, visible through his white hair. "Oh," she said, stifling a laugh. Thank the Land she wasn't an adult, then.

She turned to address the throng. "Be on your guard. Do not let the mood of this level distract you. Stick together. Only two more levels to go."

It was dusk by the time they reached the Level Six gate. GULA. Gluttony. Her stomach growled. "We're going to have to stop for the night," she said.

"I think it would be safer to stop in the next level," Rube answered, eyeing a fluttering red curtain nearby. "Good food there, too, as I recall," he added, licking his lips.

The gateway loomed over them. Once again, it was devoid of Guards. Had the Master given up trying to stop them? Somehow, she doubted it.

She was well through the gate and winding her way up a wide, cobbled boulevard when a scream pierced the air. She twisted in her saddle. "What's happened?" she asked Rube, who had been keeping pace beside her.

He scrutinised the crowd. "I'm not sure. Let me find out." He shoved his way back through the throng. Minutes dragged and the people around her started to get restless.

"Why have we stopped?" someone asked.

"I'm tired," said a young child.

"What's going on?" asked another.

Rube returned, shoving his way back to her side. She leaned down from the saddle.

"Someone died trying to pass through the gate," Rube spoke low into her ear.

Freya gasped. "They hadn't drunk the water?"

Rube shook his head. "Actually, there was more than one. Several, in fact. From what I can gather, the previous level never got its dose."

No no no no no! "That was supposed to be Amber and Di. What have they done now?" Freya demanded. Just wait until she saw them.

Rube thrust a hand through his hair. "No way of finding out right now. But what we do need to do is figure out how to stop the inhabitants of Level Five from attempting the gate."

"Or," Freya said, "we get them to drink dosed water. From another level, unless you can get your hands on more Helix water to dose their level."

"Yes," Rube said. He gripped her leg. "Leave it to me."

"I'll help, too," Hank offered.

Rube jerked his head in agreement, then addressed Freya. "By the way, there's a plaza just ahead with a big food hall in it." He indicated with his chin, then turned and thrust his way back through the crowd yelling, "Coming through."

Freya straightened and addressed the people. "We'll stop just ahead for the night and get something to eat."

"Ooh, yes, that'd be lovely," someone said.

"Do you smell that?" another asked.

Indeed, the most delicious smell had filled the air. Freya emerged into an open plaza. A large building, with a series of columns along its face, occupied the entire opposite side of the square. Beyond, people moved from one food-laden table to the next. The crowd behind her surged forward, overtaking her as they raced to the banquet hall.

"Wait. Stop!" Freya shouted.

Nobody paid her any heed.

Freya slid off Starlight. Then sighed. She'd restore order when Rube got back. She knotted the reins through an iron ring embedded in a nearby wall and trotted after the crowd.

Chapter 23

THE MASTER

"Freya. Freya. Wake up."

Somebody was shaking her. She belched softly. "Wha—?" she asked blearily. Where was she? That's right. Mmm, that had been a good meal. Her eye snapped open to reveal Rube bent over her. She jerked upright, narrowly missing his head.

He stumbled back. "Careful."

"Father," she said, rubbing her eye with the heel of her hand. "I must've fallen asleep. All that food …" She scrambled to her feet. "Are the Level Five inhabitants here?" She searched his face.

He nodded. "Yes."

"Any sign of Amber or Di?"

He closed his eyes. "No."

She straightened her breastplate and adjusted her sword and belt. "We need to keep moving. Can you help gather everyone?" She wove between the low tables, stepping over people sprawled on mats around them. Running to Starlight, she untethered him and heaved herself up into the saddle. Trotting into the centre of the square, she faced the banquet hall. "Citizens of the Golden City, you have been freed from the power of the injection—not to tarry here, but to go to Tyrelia. Come, follow me."

A few people emerged from the banquet hall, blinking in the weak sunlight. Too few.

Freya urged her mount towards the hall. "Citizens," she repeated. "I know this food is good here. I've eaten it myself. But Tyrelia also has abundant food. The Ancient provides for all people."

More people straggled out from between the columns. Still not enough. She wheeled her mount. "Freedom," she shouted, brandishing her sword. "Remember what we achieved yesterday. Some of you have come all the way from Level One. The power of the injection is broken, and you were able to pass through the gates. Some of you have fought Guards. If you want to leave the Golden City forever, you must leave now, with me. Freedom awaits."

More people ran out to join her, encouraged by Hank, Leena and young Sam, she noted. She nodded with satisfaction. She pointed Starlight's nose towards the street and spurred him onwards, Rube trotting at her side.

A low cloud hung over the City, permeated with an early morning chill. She shivered, sparing a look at the people following her. She grimaced. They were a motley crew, carrying bags, baskets and young children on their shoulders. *Not quite the army I was imagining.*

At last, the Level Seven gate loomed before her. Again, no Guards. But, as she advanced, a lone figure stepped out from the gloom, challenging her. He was clothed all in black: a swirling black robe with a hooded cowl, which hung low over his face, concealing it. He wore black leather gloves and boots, and held a black walking stick. The Master. A chill ran down Freya's spine. She froze.

"My child," he said. His voice was oil and ash. It oozed into her mind.

Freya wanted to charge him down. Defy him. Tell him she wasn't afraid. But her body refused to move. Her voice refused to speak. Her tongue stuck to the roof of her mouth. So, this was the Master. What had she expected? *Not this. Not to feel utterly terrified. Unworthy.* No. She was *not* unworthy. She had earned the Armour of Tyrelia—*that* proved her worth.

She gripped her reins and dug her heels into Starlight's flanks. *I am worthy.*

"Yah!" she cried and bounded forwards. On the other side, she reined to a halt, trembling and sweating.

Rube ran up to her. "What was that about?" he asked.

Freya blinked. "What? You didn't see him?" she asked.

"Who?"

"Why, the Master, of course."

"No," Rube said. "There was nobody there."

Subdued, Freya wended her way through the Level Seven streets to the Law Pillar, her jaw clenched. There she stopped and waited for the people to catch up. They formed a crowd around her, now hundreds strong. Rube climbed onto the plinth that formed the base of the pillar. Freya called for quiet. "Friends," she said. "The time has come. I will need you to form groups of maximum ten people. Then I will warp those groups out of the Golden City."

A gasp went up, and the crowd fell back.

"It's okay," Freya said. "It's nothing to be afraid of, but it might make you feel a little woozy."

A woman, a look of pure fear in her eyes, pointed at Freya with a shaking arm. No, not at Freya. Behind Freya.

Freya twisted in her saddle. A figure clothed completely in black stalked towards her. His face was concealed by a black hood. A black cloak billowed behind him and he wielded a black staff.

Complete silence descended over the crowd. Her heart thumped and, instinctively, Freya's eye flicked to the topmost turret of the Master's mansion, searching for a flaming arrow. The sky was empty. "Do you see him now?" she asked Rube. But from the way he stiffened at her side, she knew he did.

"Freya," the Master oozed, "you foolish girl. How do you think you'll be able to rescue all these people, when you couldn't even save Saff?"

It was as if she'd been slapped in the face. "I—I—" she stammered.

The Master tutted. He took a step towards her. "His blood isn't the first to stain your hands, either. What about all the people who died just yesterday, trying to get through the gates?"

She hung her head. Their deaths were her fault. She'd led them here. The Master was right.

"And your mother," he added.

Her heart lurched. "My mother?"

"His wife," he said nonchalantly, jabbing his staff towards Rube. "If you hadn't been born, she wouldn't have died."

A sob escaped her lips. It was true. It was *all* true. So, this was it. This was how it was going to end. They had come so far, for nothing.

Dread seeped through her. No, not dread. Apathy. There was absolutely no point in trying to leave. She would not succeed. She knew it. She sagged in her saddle. Her head drooped with the weight of the helmet and she struggled to hold her shield up.

The Master grew in stature as he took a step towards her. He flicked his free hand in some sort of signal, and she stared in horror as a flaming arrow shot from the topmost turret of his mansion. *Just like her dream.* With difficulty she dragged her shield up to cover her face. Just in time. The arrow struck the shield a bare inch from its edge. She frowned at it. It was so hard to think. Why did she have a shield?

She waded through the treacle of her mind, trying to remember. Something about having armour and an army. Was she in a battle? *Battle.* That's right, someone had said something about a battle. *Brother Nyx.* She straightened her back. The armour felt a bit lighter. She lifted her head. A flicker caught her eye. *Another arrow!* Coming straight at her. Reflexively, she swept her shield in front of her. Easier this time. *Thud.* The flaming missile struck the shield and stayed there, quivering.

"You fool," the Master sneered. "How can you possibly think to defeat me, when you've failed so many times before?" He laughed, but the sound lacked power.

Failure. The word resonated through the treacle, beating it back, loosening its hold. Brother Nyx had said something about failure. That she was only a failure if she gave up. She shook her head. "I will not give up."

It came out in a whisper. But the weight of her armour lessened, and the Master took a pace back and seemed to shrink. He cupped his ear.

"What? I can't hear you. What sort of general leads their army into battle with whispers?" he mocked, his voice edged with hysteria.

Battle. What was it Brother Nyx had said? That this was not a battle for land or wealth, but for truth. *Truth!* The treacle dissolved and was replaced with blinding certainty. The Master was the Master of Lies and he had no power over her. She did not need to defeat him, because he had already been defeated.

Spying another arrow, she cried out in a strong voice, "You have been defeated by the Ancient!" As she spoke the word 'Ancient', the arrow exploded mid-air, showering embers onto the Master. *Yes.* The Ancient *was* more powerful than the Master.

Wrenching the burning arrows out of her shield, she flung them at the Master's feet. But now, instead of a menacing, powerful presence, he was a shrivelled, creeping thing. Her mouth curled in disdain. Freya threw her arm in his direction and addressed the crowd. "This?" she exclaimed. "You're afraid of this? He is nothing!"

The woman—the one who had earlier pointed in terror at the Master—clung in fear to her neighbour, shaking her head in denial.

"Use your sword," someone yelled.

"Kill him," called another.

Freya hesitated. Maybe she could kill him. But … She lifted her chin. "I don't need to kill the Master," she said in a loud voice, "because he's already been defeated by the Ancient. So, ignore him, and come with me, if you believe." She sheathed her sword and slid off Starlight.

"He's just a shrivelled up old man," the woman declared.

The Master melted into the shadows. "That's right." Freya nodded. "Now you can see the truth. Come." She held out a hand.

The woman beckoned her family forward. "It's okay," she said. "The Girl speaks the truth."

"Stop," cried a voice from the back of the crowd.

Freya paused. She knew that voice. Jack. She craned her neck.

A ripple ran through the crowd as people were jostled and pushed from the rear. Shouts rang through the air as fighting broke out.

"It's the Guards," someone said. "Help, help."

The crowd pressed towards Freya, pinning her up against the pillar. Starlight whinnied and stamped his hooves, agitated. The woman dove out of the way of the frightened animal, dragging her children with her.

"Rube, Hank, help me get back on Starlight," Freya gasped.

Rube grabbed Starlight's reins, whilst Hank squeezed himself between Freya and the horse. Wrapping his strong arms around her small frame, he boosted Freya into the saddle.

Freya took a deep breath. "People of the Golden City," she shouted. But her voice was drowned out in the commotion.

Just then, the crowd parted to reveal several swarthy Guards hacking their way towards her. *No.* "Watch out," she yelled as she directed Starlight towards this new threat. Once again, she noted the Guards' grey pallor. *Rotten.* It dawned on her as she bore down on them: like the Master, they were a lie. This was their true form. They were not mighty beings, but weak puppets, completely subservient to the Master. And if the Master held no power over her, then neither did the Guards. Without remorse, she trampled them underfoot.

Breathing rapidly, she searched the melee for more Guards. Instead, her eyes found Jack's as he shoved his way towards her. He was flanked by two burly young men with spiky blonde hair.

"Jack, what are you doing?" Freya demanded.

"What am *I* doing? I'm stopping you from ruining the Golden City. It needs all these people for it to work."

"But these people don't *want* to stay in the Golden City. Unlike you," she flung back at him.

"Too bad if they don't want to stay. They're just going to have to."

"What do you mean? You can't stop me."

"That's what you think." Jack smirked.

Freya whipped her head up as cries of distress broke out around her. Whilst Jack had been distracting her, hundreds of Guards had encircled her group. She watched in dismay as they started grabbing inhabitants and dragging them away.

"No," she shouted, and urged Starlight towards the rear of the crowd. But she was just one girl, and the Guards were too many. The heaving crowd pressed and surged around her, hampering her movements. "Come to the pillar," she said. "Leave this place." But her shouts were swallowed up in the noise. She closed her eyes. What was she going to do?

Suddenly, a cheer went up from the direction of the pillar. She spun her mount. There! A flash of green. Then a flash of yellow. One by one, shimmering shapes emerged from a haze surrounding the pillar. The Adelphi had arrived. Relief washed through her. She was not alone. Her brothers and sisters were here. The Adelphi started gathering groups of people, and, in the blink of an eye, whisked them away.

With renewed determination, Freya wheeled her mount. "Fight the Guards, people of the Golden City," she yelled. "Head to the pillar if you want to leave." Somehow, this time, they heard her. She broke through the line of Guards and galloped around behind them, brandishing her sword. Starlight reared, kicking out at Guards as she passed. She slashed her sword, injuring more. "In the name of the Ancient, who rules Tyrelia, be free," she shouted. The people wrenched themselves from their captors' grips and raced towards the pillar. In moments, they were all gone.

Freya galloped to the pillar. Only Rube and Thyst remained. She slid off Starlight. "I'm sorry I can't take you with me," she whispered, pressing her face to her mount's. Then with one last glance at the Level Seven plaza, strewn with bodies, she gripped Rube and Thyst's hands and warped them to the Shady Desert.

~

Freya, Thyst and Rube appeared adjacent to the obelisk into a babbling crowd of citizens of the Golden City. Willow and Alex ran up to them.

"We're the last," Freya confirmed.

"How do we get all these people into Tyrelia?" Willow asked.

"Brother Nyx told me he believes there is an underground tunnel that leads towards the Zeta Gate," Freya said. "From the maps I saw, it would be north-east from here."

"You mean in that direction?" Alex asked, pointing.

"That would be about right," Rube said. "Well done, lad. You have a good sense of direction."

"That wasn't why I pointed that way. It's just … come and see for yourselves." He dashed off, ducking and weaving between groups of people.

Emerging from the crowds, Freya found Alex standing staring at the ground. Her gaze leapt to what he was looking at. "What is it?" she asked, moving to stand next him.

"A sink hole," he said. "And a tunnel." He pointed.

A tumble of earth and rocks disappeared into the gaping cavity. Freya pulled out her talking stone. Illuminating it, she crouched down, shining it into the hole. Sure enough, a tunnel led away from the rockfall. "I guess this is the way." She stood upright, then stiffened.

"What is it?" Rube asked.

"Brother Nyx said he was going to lead my parents to Tyrelia. Do you think this has anything to do with them?" She clutched at his robes.

Rube placed his hands on her shoulders. "Tell you what. I'll get a few people together and we'll do a search. The Adelphi should gather the rest of the people and guide them through the tunnel to Tyrelia."

"The Adelphi," Freya echoed. She turned to Thyst, Alex and Willow. "How did you all know to come back to the Golden City? I mean, I'm glad you did, but it was just in time."

They exchanged glances. "It was Peri and Turq who alerted us, actually," Thyst said. "They returned to Adelpha hours after the rest of us. We had been wondering where they were, but we never got a chance to find out. They burst into the Temple, shouting, asking us all to help you immediately. We all scrambled to return to Level Seven. And … you know the rest."

Alex cleared his throat. "Actually, I did manage to ask them. Apparently, they made Amber and Di swap levels with them. So, the guys went to Level Five—the one Brother Rube told them not to go to. They said they lost track of time there."

Rube narrowed his eyes and clenched his fists. He exchanged a look with Freya. "Well, that explains why the Level Five well never received its dose."

At the confused look on the faces of the others, Freya clarified. "Several Level Five citizens lost their lives attempting the gate to Level Six, before we realised the reason why." She clasped her hands and hung her head. "Such a tragedy."

They were all silent for a moment. Then Rube cleared his throat. "Freya, we need to keep moving. Are you ready to gather the people?"

She sniffed. "Yes, of course."

Rube headed off with Hank and Thyst towards the obelisk.

Freya unslung her shield and unsheathed her sword. Holding the shield aloft, she whacked it with her sword until she had the attention of the refugees. "People of the Golden City, we're going to lead you to Tyrelia via this tunnel. Please be careful, there's been a collapse, and you'll have to climb down this slip."

"But it's so dark," someone said.

"Don't worry, we have lights," Willow said. She clambered down the rockfall and lit up her stone. A green glow illuminated the space.

"Wow," a young boy said. "That's cool."

The Adelphi ushered the people in groups of forty down into the tunnel, each one holding up their stone to shed some light. Only one group remained when Rube, Hank and Thyst returned.

Thyst shot a look at Rube, then called to the group. "Alright everyone, follow me." She picked her way down the rockfall.

Rube drew Freya aside. "Freya—"

"What is it? What's wrong?" Rube looked so serious.

Rube placed his hands on Freya's shoulders. "We managed to get to the other side of the collapse."

"And?"

Rube squeezed her shoulders. "I found Brother Nyx's body under the rubble," he said gently.

Freya clapped a hand to her mouth. Suddenly, she couldn't breathe. Her vision swam. She stumbled backwards. "No," she moaned. She jerked her chin up. "My parents?"

Rube shook his head. "I don't know, Freya. I couldn't find them, but …"

He didn't need to say it. She knew. It didn't mean they weren't there. She spun and ran off into the desert, great sobs wracking her body.

Chapter 24

FREEDOM

Her heart was empty. Brother Nyx, gone. Saff, gone. Her parents, gone. Her brother—still in the Golden City. She dashed away another tear and continued stumbling down the dark tunnel, her glowing stone held out before her.

Somehow, she made it through the tunnel. Somehow, she led the people across the bridge and up the other side. She didn't remember any of it. As she climbed the final step to crest the lip of the cliff, she sank wearily to her knees.

"Freya!"

The voice sounded familiar. She raised her head.

"Freya," the call came again.

Something clicked. "Ma?" she asked, scanning the faces surrounding her. She leapt to her feet. "Ma?" she repeated.

Two people parted to reveal Martha making a beeline towards her, Thomas limping in her wake. "Freya," she cried, her arms outstretched.

"Ma, Da. You're alive." Freya threw herself into her mother's arms.

The dam of exhaustion and loneliness broke, and tears washed down her cheeks.

Martha patted her back, making soothing noises. "Of course we are, dear," she crooned. "You took an awfully long time to show up, though. We've been waiting all day."

Freya wiped her cheeks and sniffed. "We found Brother Nyx's body under a pile of rubble back at the obelisk, and I thought …" Tears threatened to flow once more.

"Hush, now," Martha said. "We're fine. Well, your da's hurt his knee, but mostly we're fine. But Brother Nyx … I'm so sorry." She stroked Freya's hair. "Now, what are you going to do about all these people?" she asked brightly, releasing her.

It was as if she surfaced after being underwater for a very long time. Freya blinked at the people milling around her. Where had they come from? Oh, that's right, the Golden City. She tossed her head, clearing it. The other Adelphi were grouped near the archway. She ran over to them.

Willow looked up as she approached. Her eyes filled with concern as she took in Freya's tear-streaked face. "Hey kiddo, are you okay?" she asked.

Freya smiled. "Yeah, I am now. Where are we going to take all these people?" she asked.

"We've just been discussing that," Rube said. "Apparently Brother Nyx had said something about taking them to Heneva and there being some sort of housing service there."

"Good, let's do it. Thyst and Rube, are you alright staying here? Just because, you know, you can't warp yet …" Her cheeks burned.

"Sure, Freya," Thyst said. "But what about them?" She flicked her eyes towards a group of people standing in a row.

"What are they doing?" Freya asked. Then it dawned on her. She'd seen people standing like that before: but that time it had been Saff and Thyst, all those weeks ago when she'd entered Tyrelia for the very first time. They, too, had stood at the top of the cliff, their entry into Tyrelia blocked by the Wall. "They can't see Tyrelia," Freya stated.

"Doesn't look like it," Thyst said. "Do you want me to talk to them?"

"No, it's okay. I'll do it."

They jumped as Freya seemingly appeared out of the Wall. "Where did everyone go?" a man asked.

"Where is this fabled Tyrelia?" asked another.

Freya gestured expansively behind her. "Why, it's right here. You just need to believe in the Ancient, and you'll see it." She stepped back through the Wall.

"Where did she go?" a woman asked.

Freya re-joined them. "I just went into Tyrelia. As I said, it's right here."

The woman screwed up her face. "Sorry love. All your appearing and disappearing is making me dizzy."

A man thumped his fist on the Wall. "This here Wall is as solid as ever. You've brought us here for nothing."

"Yeah," someone else agreed. "Why did you bring us to this forlorn place? We're in the middle of nowhere. We were better off in the Golden City."

"Please," Freya begged, "you just need to believe in the Ancient. Then you'll see."

"Can you tell us more about this Ancient?" a woman asked.

"Take us back," a man growled.

"Yes, take us back," another repeated.

Freya stared at them, dumbstruck. How could someone want to go back there, after everything that had happened? She sought Rube. "Rube. I need help. Some of these people have asked for more explanation about the Ancient. But the rest want me to take them back to the Golden City. What should I do?"

Rube ran a hand through his hair. "There's nothing else you can do, Freya. They'll have to be taken back. A job for Peri and Turq I reckon. Willow, Peri, Turq!" He hailed the three Adelphi, indicating the group that was unable to pass through the Wall. "Willow, can you talk to those people about Tyrelia, please? Peri and Turq, can you please warp these others back to the Golden City?"

Rube slung his arm around Freya's shoulders, leading her towards the Zeta gate. "And that is why we don't warp people straight to the Law Pillars in Tyrelia," he commented.

Moments later, Willow joined them with the group she'd spoken to. They were gazing about in wonder. "Come with me, and I'll take you to your new homes," Willow said. She led them to the Zeta pillar and, in a blink, they were gone.

Freya hailed her parents, who were sitting on the grass nearby with Thyst.

"Now what, Freya?" Martha asked.

Freya hauled her parents to their feet, then wriggled between them. "Now, I take you to Adelpha," she said. "Rube, Thyst, hold on."

In a blink, they were there. The last rays of sun lingered on the tips of the mountains ringing the valley. The forest leaves rustled in a gentle breeze and birds twittered as they hunted insects in the gathering dusk.

Freya hurried towards the Temple, expecting—willing— Brother Nyx to fling open the doors and hobble out on to the steps. But the building remained silent. Freya gulped. "Everyone, this is the Temple of the Adelphi. This is where I've been living the past three weeks, training."

She trotted up the stairs and flung open the tall doors. She ran to the rear of the room and gestured at the poem. "This is the poem about the Armour of Tyrelia," she said.

From behind her, someone gasped.

"What is it?" she asked, turning.

Thyst pointed. "Your armour," she said. "It's gone."

So it had. She raised her eyebrows at Rube.

He shrugged. "I guess the task has been fulfilled. The quest is completed, and the Armour is no longer needed," he said.

"I guess so," she echoed.

Just then, the others burst into the atrium, chattering and laughing. "Freya," Willow said. "There you are." She ran up to her and gathered her in a hug, swinging her off her feet.

"Put me down," Freya giggled.

"We did it," Willow declared.

Alex whooped. "Hey," he said, looking Freya up and down. "What have you done with the Armour?"

"It's gone," she said simply.

Alex eyed her thoughtfully. "It's not really gone, though," he said.

"What do you mean?" Freya asked.

"Well, you earned it by passing all those tests. You led all those people out of Medar. You spoke up when you needed to—you confronted the Master. You were brave and strong. The Armour may have physically disappeared, but I think it's still really there inside you."

Their eyes locked. Freya's heartbeat thrummed in her ears. She wasn't aware of it happening, but somehow Alex was holding her hand. It felt good.

Somebody whistled. "About time," Willow said.

Freya jumped, blushing furiously, and tore her eyes off Alex. But she didn't let go of his hand.

"Where's Brother Nyx?" Peri asked. He was back fast. He must've warped straight back to Adelpha after returning the people to the Golden City.

"Ah, he's gone," Rube said.

"Where did he go?" asked Peri.

"He gave his life to save ours," Martha said quietly.

"Oh."

"We should hold some sort of ceremony," Willow suggested, dashing away a tear. "You know, to remember him."

"Yes." Freya sniffed. She let go of Alex's hand and leaned over to squeeze Willow's shoulder.

"We should name someone to take his place," Alex suggested.

"I guess so," Freya said. "But his replacement is supposed to get his onyx stone and take the name Nyx. That might be a bit tricky given that his stone is lost."

Martha coughed. "Actually, his stone isn't lost. He gave it to us for safe keeping. It's here." She held it out.

Freya stared at Martha in wonder. "He must've known," she murmured.

"Perhaps he did," Rube agreed.

They all trooped outside and gathered in a semi-circle around the Law Pillar. It seemed the right thing to do. Hilda joined them. Freya laced her fingers and bowed her head. "I didn't know him for very long, but Brother Nyx changed my life. I first knew of him as the hermit. Then when I met him, I thought maybe he was the Ancient himself—" She felt her cheeks grow hot at this admission "—but as it turned out, he was the head of the Ancient Order of the Adelphi. He was gentle, kind, fair and above all, wise."

"Yes," Willow added, "and very old." She grinned.

"Yes, and old," Freya agreed. "But today, his watch is done. And now, I name Brother Rube to be our new leader."

"Yes, Brother Rube," the others cheered. They pulled out

their stones and held them aloft, imbuing them with light as they did so. A rainbow of colours glowed from their hands. "Brother Nyx. Our new leader."

"Long live the Adelphi!"

Epilogue

THE QUEST CONTINUES

"Where shall we go today?" Willow asked.

"There's somewhere I've been wanting to go for a while," Freya replied.

"Where's that then?"

"It's where I used to live in Medar. A place called Nob."

Martha was helping Hilda clear the breakfast dishes. "Can you take me too, dear?" she asked. "I'd love to tell my sister and friends about this place."

"That's a really good idea," Freya enthused. "Do you think Da will want to come too? We could make it a family outing." She smiled.

"I'll ask him," Martha said.

While she was gone, Freya mused, "You know, when we rescued all those people from the Golden City and brought them back here, I thought our work was done. But really, it was just the beginning."

Willow clapped her on the shoulder. "Too right. Last week we rescued all those Cave People. Today perhaps some people from Nob. The best part is, we get to go on a new quest every day. What job could beat that?"

THE END

Dear Reader,

Thank you for reading my story. Perhaps you are wondering why I dedicated this book to 'everyone trapped in Medar', when it is clearly a made-up place. Well, it's not. The *Realm Trilogy* books are allegorical, and are a representation of the world we live in. I believe there is more to life than meets the eye. There is another dimension. Tyrelia is real. You just need to believe to be able to experience it.

If you'd like to find out more, please feel free to email me at **realmtrilogy@gmail.com** or check out this youtube video: **https://www.youtube.com/watch?v=q3evfrAtQmA**

If you enjoyed this book and the others from the trilogy, I'd really appreciate it if you could leave a review. Having reviews is really important and helpful for others who are considering reading this story.

You can leave a review on Amazon via this link:

https://www.amazon.com/review/create-review/ref=cm_cr_arp_d_wr_but_lft?ie=UTF8&channel=reviews-product&asin=B08GJYT9WD

or on Goodreads.

Also, if you're as taken with the message of this book as I am, why not lend your copy to your friends or buy the book as a present? I hope you agree that it is a story worth sharing.

Sharon Manssen

October 2020

TYRELIA (poem revealed in Medar)

Tyrelia! Land of gold
A land so lovely to behold
O, land of beauty, land of light
Joyous refuge, pure delight

Tyrelia! That land so fair
Of meadows green and clean pure air
Of stately trees in forests vast
Of ancient rocks from ages past

Majestic mountains, white with snow
Their crystal tears to rivers flow
Splashing sparkles dance up high
Painting rainbows in the sky

Swathes of splendid floral hues
The land with colour do imbue
The golden sun smiles down from high
As he marches 'cross the sky

As flaming sunset turns to night
Stars and moon cast silver light
On all who choose to live lives free
From the Master's tyranny

He has no claim to any throne
He long ago was overthrown
By the Ancient, true and just
In whom all living things can trust

Who alone has claim to rule
Tyrelia, beyond the Wall
Tyrelia! O, land of gold
O, land so lovely to behold

TYRELIA *(poem revealed in Tyrelia)*

Tyrelia! Land of gold
A land so lovely to behold
O, land of beauty, land of light
Joyous refuge, pure delight

Tyrelia! That land so fair
Of meadows green and clean pure air
Of stately trees in forests vast
Of ancient rocks from ages past

Fresh clean air, sparkling waters
Quench your thirst, sons and daughters
Head to the place with sulphurous steam
To free Medar from the Master's schemes

Go up Helix River, to its source
At the waterfall—a powerful force—
Follow the sounds of birds up high
Of honey bees buzzing as they fly

When sunlight fades to shades of grey
At dusk watch for nature's display
From whence the cloud comes, will reveal
The path which is elsewise concealed

Deep within the mountain rift
Find the hermit to claim your gift
He will guide you in your task
You won't receive if you don't ask.

Acknowledgements

Wow. I can't believe I finished the story. It was a really strange feeling when I penned the final words of my first draft back in September 2019, after carrying the story around inside me for over fifteen years. I would never have got there without the support of my wonderful husband, Craig. He allowed me to spend weekends beavering away on writing, instead of spending the time with him. Thank you. Thanks also to my children, Lucas and Sarah. You tolerated my endless discussions on story ideas and have helped shape the story in so many ways. Also, thanks to Grace Bridges, whose presentation on the Snowflake Method at the Geysercon writers' conference inspired me to try this method for plotting this novel. It worked so well! Also, thanks to my idol and friend, Lee Murray, who not only provided valued guidance on the manuscript, but has also given me so many opportunities to grow and network in the Bay of Plenty writing scene. You are awesome! And to my editor Chad Dick of 100% Proof Ltd – thank you for your suggestions with my story arc (especially the exploding arrow!) and your eagle eye. Finally, thanks to my beta readers for wading through early drafts and providing valuable suggestions: Eva, Abbie, Lenna and especially Karen and Gerardine. I could not have done this without your fabulous input and constant support. Thank you all so much!

Sharon Manssen
October 2020

About the Author

A fantasy fan since being read 'The Hobbit' by her father at the fireside at the age of six, she has been an avid bookworm her entire life. When the idea for her current trilogy popped into her head, there was never any doubt that it would be in the fantasy genre. Unfortunately, real life gets in the way, and writing has to fit around her full-time job at a global engineering consultancy and family life (husband and two young adult children). It took ten years to pen her first book, Medar, which was a finalist for the Tom Fitzgibbon Award in 2015 and was published in 2017. Her second book, Tyrelia was nominated in the Young Adult Fiction category in the 2019 Sir Julius Vogel Awards.

Other books by S R Manssen

Medar – Realm Trilogy Book One

Tyrelia – Realm Trilogy Book Two

Connect with me

I hope you enjoyed reading my book as much as I enjoyed writing it. You can follow me on these social media platforms:

Website	http://www.srmanssen.com
Facebook	https://www.facebook.com/realmtrilogy/
Smashwords	https://www.smashwords.com/profile/view/SharonManssen
LinkedIn	https://www.linkedin.com/in/sharon-manssen/
Email	realmtrilogy@gmail.com